UNDER ATTACK!

On a sudden impulse, Jay ran to the rear door, let himself out and crossed the adjoining platforms to the first passenger coach in one quick bound.

"We're under attack!" he yelled to the full coach. A woman stifled a scream, and the coach erupted in a clamor of excited talk. Everyone was crowding the windows.

"What was that explosion?" one man asked.

"They unhitched the engine and pulled it across the bridge and then dynamited the bridge. We're isolated. Any of you men who are armed and want to help defend this train, get up to the express car—quick!"

Three men got up and started forward. Jay ran down the aisle toward the next car. He shouted his message in the second car and got two recruits. He sent one of them to the Pullman and caboose to spread the word.

He dared waste no more time. He had taken only a couple of minutes, but it may have been too much.

Six men were crowded at the door of the first passenger coach, waiting for him. Just as he reached them, a gun boomed outside and glass exploded somewhere ahead. The men turned to stare at him.

"The express car's locked," one said, peering out the door. "One of 'em just put a slug through the side window." Jay ground his teeth. They were trapped outside the express car.

Other *Leisure* books by Tim Champlin:
SWIFT THUNDER

FLYING EAGLE

TIM CHAMPLIN

LEISURE BOOKS   NEW YORK CITY

For Gordon Shirreffs and Mary Ann Eckels

A LEISURE BOOK®

November 2001

Published by special arrangement with Golden West Literary Agency.

Dorchester Publishing Co., Inc.
276 Fifth Avenue
New York, NY 10001

ISBN 0-8439-4937-6

The name "Leisure Books" and the stylized "L" with design are trademarks of Dorchester Publishing Co., Inc.

Printed in the United States of America.

Visit us on the web at www.dorchesterpub.com.

FLYING EAGLE

Chapter One

Jay McGraw stared upward at the man who dangled in the sky more than a thousand feet above him. Jay's mouth was dry and his heart pounding as he watched the tiny figure climbing down a rope hanging from the wicker basket of a tethered gas balloon. The man was reaching with his feet for a tiny, swing-type seat suspended a few feet below the basket.

"Wish I'd brought my field glasses," Fred Casey muttered, shading his eyes. Casey, dressed in the dark blue uniform of a San Francisco policeman, stood on the other side of Jay and shared his fascination at this amazing sight.

"OOOHHH!!" A collective gasp from the crowd focused the attention on the aeronaut high above them. The man was clinging to the knotted rope, his feet kicking free as he twisted helplessly. The wind off the bay was gusting. The balloon strained against its long mooring, and the suspended seat was blowing away from him.

Jay could see clearly the figure of a giant eagle with outspread wings painted on the surface of the balloon. He swallowed the lump in his throat. How long could the man's arms hold him against the force of the wind and the pull of his own weight?

The figure far above them was slowly working his way downward, reaching with his feet for the tiny, elusive seat. But the wind was twisting it away from him. Finally, the seat swung close enough for the man to snag it with his foot. Very slowly he was able to pull it near enough to shift his weight, reach from the rope to the lines holding the seat, and swivel himself into a sitting position. He sat there for another minute or two, either to rest or to wait for the late afternoon wind to subside. He used the time to adjust the straps of his parachute harness.

A hush fell on the crowd as he took a long line in his hand and pulled, opening the rip panel in the top of the balloon. Gas escaped and the balloon began to drop, creating momentum to partially fill the yellow silk parachute. The balloon had pivoted into the bay breeze, adding wind to the inflating silk.

With the parachute partially inflated, the man jumped.

"OOOHHH!!" the crowd gasped as the figure plummeted downward. The parachute filled and buoyed him up. The taut, yellow silk seemed to hang against the blue sky, but then could be seen sweeping in great, arcing swings toward the grass of Golden Gate Park.

Jay let out his breath in a rush and joined the surge of the crowd toward the open spot where the aeronaut was coming down. As the man struck the ground and rolled over, the yellow silk collapsing downwind of him, the crowd broke into spontaneous applause. Jay's eyes shifted to some of the faces around him. How many of these men and women were thrill-seekers who had come here to see a foolhardy daredevil leap to his death from this balloon? But he saw no disappointment—only excitement and pleasure at the jump and safe landing.

The crowd swarmed around the aeronaut before he could even get out of his harness. Jay McGraw and Fred Casey ran toward him, but they knew they could never get close to the balloonist as the crowd pressed in. In the crush of excitement, people were pressing against him from all sides: men in bowler hats and black suits, women in their long dresses, wide hats and capes to shut out the chill of the early autumn breeze.

Jay lost Fred Casey in the crowd. He was gone. Then he spotted his friend running through the outer edges of the group, chasing a short man in a slouch hat who was ducking and dodging some ten yards ahead of him. A woman screamed as she was knocked aside. The small man broke free of the crowd and sprinted out across the grassy field with Casey right behind him. The taller policeman rapidly overtook the fleeing man and Jay watched in amazement as Fred launched himself in a perfect flying tackle at the back of the fleeing man's legs and brought him down cleanly.

Jay moved away from the crowd as fast as he could and came running up as Casey was snapping his handcuffs on the smaller man.

"Marvin Cutter," Casey said, "one of the more notorious pickpockets in the city." He pulled the man to his feet, and Jay looked into the narrow face that was covered with black stubble. Lank, black hair hung down into the man's eyes. His sack coat sagged open, heavily.

With a deft motion, Casey reached inside the coat and withdrew a calf-skin purse. "Ah, taken to carrying ladies' handbags, now, have you?" he said, holding it up. Cutter stared at him stonily and made no reply. "Better check to see if you have your billfold," Casey said over his shoulder.

McGraw patted his hip pocket. "It's gone!"

"Yeah. I saw him brush up against you in the crowd. Figgered he got it."

By the time Casey had frisked the thief, he had four billfolds on the ground at his feet and a small, curious crowd was gathering.

"You must like it in jail, Marvin," Casey said. "Do you keep doing this just so you can get free room and board? One of these days, the judge is going to put you away for a long time."

"Fred, I had an entire week's pay in here," Jay said, accepting the billfold the policeman handed him. "Don't know what I'd do without you. Guess I need you around to take care of me," he said, grinning ruefully.

"After you've been in police work for a few years, watching for things like this is just second nature," the mustachioed Casey replied. "I'd better get Mr. Cutter to the station house," he added, stuffing the remainder of the leather billfolds into his side coat pockets. "I have to get back to my beat in Chinatown."

Jay took a last look at the face of Marvin Cutter. The pickpocket did not seem fearful, angry, remorseful, or depressed. The narrow, stubbled face of the thief seemed placid, resigned, as if this were all in a day's work. You take your chances while plying your trade, make a profit or you get caught. As Fred Casey led Cutter away, Jay thought that this must be a routine happening for an habitual petty criminal.

This man could have made more today than the $1,000 that aeronaut got for that parachute jump, if he had gotten away, Jay thought as he moved through the thinning crowd toward the rented rig he had parked in a nearby grove of trees.

He knew the promoter paid the balloonist a dollar a foot and also knew he wouldn't have done it for a million dollars.

Jay glanced back at the solid knot of people still packed around the aeronaut. His assistants were busy cranking in the mooring line that held the balloon. The daredevil was going to lecture at the Civic Auditorium tonight.

San Francisco, in 1883, was a free-wheeling city of extravagant wealth where even housemaids were seen to wear gold jewelry. It was a city where people took it for granted that nothing—no scheme or feat—was too outrageous to try. A pioneer spirit of independence, danger and survival prevailed.

Thus, the sight of a man flying a balloon in the sky captivated the imagination of many, including Jay McGraw who, just a year earlier, had arrived in California from the Midwest by way of the Arizona Territory. After escaping near-death at the hands of the Chinatown tongs during a robbery of the U.S. Mint, he had joined the Wells Fargo Co. as a messenger.

As he drove the rented rig back to the livery, he thought of how routine and boring his job had become in the past few months in comparison to the thrilling life of an aeronaut. Jay made up his mind to attend the balloonist's lecture that night. At least he could share vicariously in some adventures before starting his routine run to Chicago the next day.

Chapter Two

"What are you looking so glum about?" Jay inquired of Fred Casey as the policeman slid into the booth opposite him the next morning. The lean, handsome Casey was dressed in his best gray suit and vest, and had just come from ten o'clock Mass at the Mission Dolores, a few blocks away. It had been their habit, over the past several months, when neither of these two young bachelors was working, to meet every Sunday morning at Mitchell's Restaurant for an early lunch. The food here was tasty, but not expensive.

"I just saw Dick Benson at church, and he told me the thief, Marvin Cutter, escaped from jail late last night," he replied, frowning. "Somebody down there was mighty careless. It was hardly worth my time and trouble bringing him in."

"Well, at least you recovered all the stuff he took," Jay said.

Casey nodded. "But he's probably already back on the street somewhere, relieving people of their valuables. He's one of the slickest I've ever seen."

A balding, white-aproned waiter sauntered over with a pot of coffee and two heavy mugs. Jay ordered a small steak and potatoes and Casey, ham and eggs and toast. The waiter nodded and disappeared.

Casey shrugged and looked out the window beside him at the bright sunlight reflecting off a red and gold cable car rattling up the street. "Well,

Cutter's not my problem now. I have other things to think about."

"Such as?" Jay asked, stirring a dash of cream into his coffee.

"Benson also told me there's a message waiting for me at my boardinghouse to report to the station house for some overtime work."

"Oh? What's up?" Jay arched his brows over the rim of his cup.

"Do you know of Julian Octavian Brown?"

Jay thought for a moment. "The banker?"

"The same."

"Filthy rich, as I recall. One of the tycoons who made it big right after the big gold rush about thirty years back."

"Right. Almost on a level with Crocker and Huntington and Fair and Flood and that bunch."

"What about him?"

"He disappeared the night before last."

"Disappeared? How?"

"Don't know, exactly. He's been a widower for a long time. No children. A really odd duck, who has become a virtual recluse in that mansion of his for the past few years. Only spends a few hours each week at his bank in the city. Rumor has it that his fortune has been eroding away gradually as other banks have sprung up in competition, and his holdings in the Virginia City mines have begun to play out. Talk in the financial community is that he's made some bad personal investments, also some large loans from his bank in an attempt to recoup. And some of the borrowers have gone bankrupt and defaulted. Of course, all of this is only what I've heard and read third-hand accounts of. A lowly policeman is not privy to those financial circles."

"So the man just vanished?" Jay urged, trying to bring his friend back to the point of his tale.

Casey nodded. "His cook had the night off Friday. She came back in yesterday morning and found the old Chinese houseman murdered and Mr. Julian Octavian Brown gone. No ransom notes, no clues, no signs of a struggle. They must have taken him totally by surprise, or he would have put up a fight. Brown is a big, stocky man, in great shape for his age and not afraid of anything, they say."

"Why is your captain calling you in on this?" Jay asked, cutting the smoking steak the waiter set before him. "You're a member of the Special Chinatown squad. Isn't this a little out of your line?"

"I'm in line for promotion to detective. I've been with the force more than five years now. And that business you and I were involved in last year in recovering half of the gold from the mint robbery gave my career a big boost in the eyes of my chiefs."

"I wonder what happened to the rest of that money. A million and a half in gold double eagles—just vanished."

"I wish I knew." Casey shook his head.

"Think this will be a simple case of robbery or kidnapping?"

"Somehow I don't think so. All I know about it is what I got from Benson this morning, because it's being kept out of the papers for a day or two. But Brown's houseman wasn't just shot or stabbed. His murder has all the marks of a Chinese tong execution—his skull was split with a hatchet."

"Damn!" Jay grimaced.

"Yeah, I know. Pretty gruesome. But until now, that sort of thing has been confined to the Chinese quarter of the city to prevent stirring up trouble with the white man's law. Those tongs are great at fighting among themselves. I ought to know; I have to go down there every night and try to prevent some of it. That may be the reason they're calling me in on this case, since I have as much experience with the tongs as any white man. I just don't know what to make of it. Maybe the old Chinese houseman had some sort of ties with the tongs. But then, why would they take J. Octavian Brown? I'm pretty anxious to get down to the station and get going on this one. It sounds fascinating."

"You don't seem to be in any hurry," Jay remarked, watching Casey wiping up egg yolk with a piece of toast.

"Man can't work on an empty stomach," he replied. "If I have to work on Sunday, I'm going to take my time getting there—even if I will get paid a little extra, and might be working toward a promotion. Besides, I don't officially know they want me yet. I haven't been back to my boardinghouse to get the message."

He wiped his plate clean, took a sip of coffee, and leaned back with a sigh.

"I have to leave for Chicago this afternoon," Jay announced. "I have a turnaround trip this time, but I still won't be back for more than two weeks. You know, I've been making this run as a messenger for Wells Fargo for months now, and there are only two things I don't like about it."

"What's that?"

"I'm gone too long on these cross-country trips, and the job so far has been boring. I have to stay locked up in that express car the entire way, eating and sleeping in there, unless I slip out for a meal now and then."

Fred started to reply, but Jay held up his hand. "I'm not complaining, mind you. I really appreciate the good word you put in at Wells Fargo to help me get the job after that mint robbery business. And it pays a lot better than driving a beer wagon. I just wish . . . well, I'd like to be working with you on this disappearance case. Seems like you have all the excitement. I just lucked into that last thing. After a few runs, this messenger job has gotten pretty dull. My life was a lot more interesting and exciting when I was a temporary detective with the San Francisco Police."

Casey grunted. "Excitement! Huh! Terror, you mean. I'm surprised I've lived to be twenty-six. I don't think I want to stay in police work the rest of my life, but right now, it's the only thing I know. You've got a good future with Wells Fargo. It's one of the biggest and most respected companies in the country. And, most important, they appreciate good employees."

"Yeah. Guess I shouldn't gripe. At least by laying over in Chicago, I've been able to go over and visit my folks in Iowa a couple of times since I've had this job."

"Wish I had some family to visit," Fred said somewhat wistfully, glancing out the window. "I was an only child and my parents died when I was just a boy. Raised by my great aunt, but she's gone now. Came out here to California to seek my fortune when I was still in my teens, and got hooked up with the police department sort of by accident."

They fell silent, sipping their coffee and thinking their own thoughts.

"I got to meet that aeronaut last night after his lecture," Jay said to change the subject and head off his friend's sad mood.

"Oh, yeah? What's he like?"

"I thought he was an arrogant loudmouth. The man's a braggart. Overbearing. But he comes across on stage as confident and knowledgeable. They had a reception for him afterwards and that's where he let the mask slip."

"You really took a dislike to this fella, didn't you?"

"First and only impression. Probably never see him again."

Casey wiped his mustache with the napkin. "Guess I'd better be getting back to the boardinghouse to see if I have a message waiting for me." He belied his eagerness by pouring himself another cup of coffee from the pot on the table. The late morning sun flooded the snow-white linen table-cloth between them, glinting off the silverware. In the few seconds of ensuing silence, the clinking of glassware and the murmur of other voices drifted to their ears from the few other patrons.

A few minutes later they paid their bill and walked outside.

"I'll see you in two weeks," Jay said, shaking hands with Fred. "And I want to hear that you've solved this disappearance case when I get back," he added with a grin.

"I'll have it cleaned up by then," Casey assured him as they went their separate ways.

But, if Jay had known what he would encounter before their paths crossed again, he might very well have gone to Wells Fargo and resigned on the spot.

Chapter Three

Whenever Jay left on one of his Chicago trips, he always delayed until the last possible minute, reluctant to leave the familiar surroundings of San Francisco, the city he had come to love. He missed his friends and the social activities. But once he had locked himself into his self-imposed prison of the Wells Fargo Express Car on the eastbound Central Pacific and cut his ties, temporarily, with San Francisco, he was calm. But tearing himself away each time was a real conflict.

Finally, at five o'clock that afternoon, he tossed his bag, containing his extra clothes, through the open door of the express car and vaulted up after it, disdaining to use the steps into the end door of the wooden car. On inside, he left the big side door open to admit plenty of air and light. He stowed his bag under his built-in bunk against the opposite wall, then went through a familiar routine of checking the short, double-barrelled shotgun to be sure it was loaded before replacing it in its wooden rack. Under the rack was a small box with a hinged lid, which contained cleaning gear for the gun, some rags, and a can of oil, along with two dozen twelve-gauge shells and an equal number of shells with slugs. None of the ammunition had been used since Jay had been making this run. He knew it would probably keep almost indefinitely, but the thought went through his mind as he dropped the lid and fastened it in place, that it was about time to replace it with fresh shells, just in case. Since Wells Fargo had taken to the rails, the number of robberies had dropped off dramatically. Holdups were still frequent events on the stagecoach runs from the mining towns of Nevada and California where no trains had reached, but attempted robberies of express cars were much rarer. He read with interest every account in the newspapers of these train robberies and talked to other messengers who had actually experienced them. Two of the attempts had been successful. One instance where the robbers had penetrated the car occurred when the car was dynamited from underneath, killing the messenger. The second happened when the express car had been separated from the train after the rails were blocked and the express car set afire, forcing the messenger to open the door.

All in all, Jay McGraw began this trip feeling not only safe, but bored. He always brought plenty of reading material in the form of a book or two, and a copy of the *Police Gazette* or *Harper's Weekly* stuffed into his bag to pass the time and further his interrupted education. Two years of college had come to an abrupt halt when he ran out of money back in Iowa. But, if the truth were known, it was his love of athletics that also contributed to the end of his college career since he had begun to neglect his studies.

On the train, he routinely looked over the boxes and bags stacked in one end of the car, the freight and mail that he would ride with for the few days it would take them to reach Chicago. But what he was really assigned to guard was the famous Wells Fargo treasure box that had been the object of so many highwaymen over the past thirty years. He went to the open side door to take delivery of this box as two armed guards carried it up the platform and lifted it up to him. It was relatively small, measuring two feet by one foot by one foot, made of wood bound with iron straps, and secured with a large padlock. The box was painted green with WELLS FARGO & CO. in white lettering on one side.

"Not as heavy this time," Jay commented as he grabbed one end and slid the box inside.

"Have a good trip, McGraw," one of the guards said, handing him a large ring containing all the keys to the inside door locks on the car as well as that of the padlock on the treasure box. The old guard sauntered off without another word. It did not take the brass plate affixed to the front of their railroad caps to identify them as Wells Fargo men. Their seamed, weathered faces and white hair marked them as men who had survived many years as shotgun messengers on coaches in the far-flung reaches of the company's network in the West. They had simply grown too old to be effective, but they still needed employment. The company had rewarded their faithful service by giving them this light, relatively safe duty to perform as long as their eyes were clear and their hands still steady. The men did security duty at the Wells Fargo office next to the Oakland depot, a responsible, but less strenuous and dangerous job.

Jay swung the box inside the car and slid it against the wall. He would soon transfer its contents to the iron safe. Then, with one last look around at the Oakland platform, where a few stragglers were running for the passenger coaches, he slid the big door closed and locked it from the inside.

Two blasts on the steam whistle were followed by a muffled announcement from the conductor. He waited a minute until the train started with a jolt before lighting the coal-oil lamp that hung from the ceiling in the center of the car. The warm yellow glow spread through the car, dispelling the gloom. Some light found its way in through a series of small skylights running the length of the car on either side of a narrow, raised walkway on the roof. The only additional light came through the iron-barred windows in each sliding side door. The bottom of the glass in these windows was even with the top of his head. There was also a small, barred window in the door at each end of the car. For reading and close paperwork, a smaller lamp was clamped into a wall sconce beside his desk near the head of his bunk. He lifted the chimney and struck a match to the lamp. Then he adjusted the wick to a steady brightness before sliding open the small, roll-top desk. Instantly, he smelled the aroma of roast beef.

"Ah, she did it again," he muttered to himself, carefully removing the linen napkin and the inverted pie plate that covered another tin plate piled high with slices of roast beef and potatoes smothered in gravy, boiled carrots, and a thick wedge of cornbread with butter. A knife and fork were rolled up in another napkin beside the plate. On a torn, brown piece of wrapping paper was penciled the single word, "Nancy." When she first started leaving him meals to see him off on his trips, she had written him a short note, but lately she had simply signed her name. Nancy Fultz, a working girl from a poor family, waited tables in the cafe adjacent to the depot, where Jay had taken his meals often before boarding for his trips, and frequently upon his return. Of late he had taken to crossing on the last ferry he could get before his departure, preferring to spend as much time as possible in San Francisco before he had to go. Nancy's heart was as big as the helpings she served him on the sly. In appreciation, he always paid her even more than the meal was worth. He found her charming and personable and had taken to including her in his circle of friends in San Francisco, where her wit and sense of humor had quickly made her very popular.

He stripped off his jacket and black pillbox railroad cap and hung them on a peg, then sat down to eat while the food was still hot. His holstered gun bumped the arm of the captain's chair and he briefly considered, then rejected, the idea of hanging up his gunbelt also. He had formed the habit of keeping his revolver with him all the time when he was on duty, except when sleeping, and then it was within reach beside his bunk. This weapon was his personal revolver—a pearl-handled, nickel-plated, .38-caliber, double-action Colt Lightning. He was an excellent shot with it, and it had become part of him since he carried it constantly on the job. The weapon had been given to him more than two years before by the father of a girl he had rescued from Apaches in the Arizona Territory. Many Wells Fargo messengers carried Lightnings, so the company had had no objections to his using his own weapon. Even with five chambers loaded, it was much lighter than a big .45.

Jay concentrated on eating his meal as the express rolled east into the darkness of the Central Valley toward Sacramento. After he finished, he washed his dish at the end of the car where he pumped water from a barrel into a tin basin. Then he pumped himself a good drink of water.

He lugged the Wells Fargo chest over to the four-foot-high iron safe. He spun the dial of the lock left, then right, then left again according to a combination he'd memorized. Grabbing the handle, he gave a twist and the door opened with a dull, metallic "clunk." Then he selected a key from the ring and opened the padlock of the treasure box. The box contained a heavy leather pouch that Jay presumed contained gold coins, judging from the feel of it. There was a thick, manila envelope, sealed with sealing wax, some stacks of bonds, and bound bundles of greenbacks in denominations of twenties, fifties and hundreds. There was also a lightweight bamboo tube about six inches long by about two inches in diameter. The tube was wrapped in brown paper and had a name and address written on it. It could've contained anything from a rolled scroll to precious gems. Jay shoved it into the big safe with the cash, bonds, and leather bag, closed and locked the door, and spun the dial.

He grunted as he stood up from a squatting position, feeling the rush of blood back into his muscular legs. He heard the wail of the steam whistle as it blew for a crossing or some small town. But the train never slacked speed and his enclosed world rocked and jerked and bumped into the darkness.

Flopping down on his bunk, he kicked off his shoes and reached into his bag for a book. But, after only two pages of the novel, his eyes began to get heavy. The rocking motion and the rapid clicking of the wheels over the rail joints acted as a soporific on him. He forced himself awake and tried to concentrate on his book. It was too early to go to sleep. But after an hour he gave up. "Don't even remember what I've read," he muttered to himself, yawning mightily and putting the book under his bunk. He unhooked his Elgin watch and put it in his shoe, unstrapped his gunbelt and slid it under his bunk near his head. Then he reached up and turned down the lamp to a low glow. Ten minutes later he was rolled in his blankets and asleep.

Chapter Four

Usually, by the second day out, Jay was toughened up to the trip. And this time was no exception. By the morning of the second day they had put the major mountain ranges behind them, with the help of a second locomotive on the steep grades of the Sierras. The train these two iron horses were hauling consisted of the Wells Fargo express car that was also carrying the mail this trip, followed by two passenger coaches, a Pullman, a flatcar, and the caboose. Tied down on the flatcar, with wheels firmly chocked, were two wagons, fully loaded and covered with canvas.

The express car was equipped with a potbellied stove at the end opposite Jay's bunk, its pipe protruding through the roof. But, even though these early autumn nights in the mountains had been cold, Jay had chosen not to use it. They had crossed the high desert of northern Nevada and Utah and had chugged and panted their way through the cuts and grades of the Wasatch Range, east of Salt Lake City. Since the train carried no dining car, they had stopped for a forty-minute lunch break at Rock Springs, Wyoming Territory.

Jay consumed an antelope steak and potatoes at the depot restaurant. As he came back out, a toothpick between his teeth, a chill, northwest wind penetrated the white cotton shirt he wore. He glanced at the sky. Dark, ragged clouds were scudding overhead. The conductor was calling for everyone to board and the passengers were hurrying to reclaim their seats. Far out over the plain, Jay saw a formation of a flight of wild ducks, heading south with a strong tailwind. Above the wind, he thought he could even hear their faint cries. He watched, fascinated, until they blended into the darkened sky to the southeast. Then he hopped the forward end platform of his car and let himself in with his key, locking the door behind him.

Dropping into the chair at his desk, he sighed and picked up a magazine. How often he wished he could ride the cupola of the caboose like the conductor did and, at least, get a good view of the passing countryside. Even on a dreary day like this, it would be better than being locked up where he could see nothing. When the train was moving, he often let himself out onto the rear platform of his car and stood, hanging onto the iron railing, breathing the air, tainted with smoke and ash from the locomotive, and felt the welcome wind whipping his face. He was not a person who could stand to be indoors most of the time. It would be next to impossible for him to work in an office every day, especially where he had to wear a coat and tie and answer to some hard-nosed boss. Occasionally, he even walked back through the passenger coaches, not only for the exercise, but also to get a look at the passengers. When he had done this the previous day he had seen a face he recognized, although it took him a few minutes to remember the man after he had passed on down the aisle and exited the back of the coach. It was Fletcher Hall, the aeronaut. Now, as he sat staring blankly at the magazine page, he wondered what that arrogant individual was doing on his train. Without realizing it, Jay had taken to assuming a possessive air about this train. Any train he rode as Wells Fargo messenger, he thought of as *his*, even though he had responsibility for only one car and its contents. This express was bound for Chicago with only short stops along the way, so Jay had to assume the man was returning to the East or Middle West with his gas balloon, carboys of acid, wooden kegs of iron filings, and other equipment. In fact, Jay suddenly realized, the two wagons on the flatcar must contain the deflated gas envelope, the lines, and all the paraphernalia needed to get one of those big gasbags aloft and put on a show such as the one he had seen in San Francisco. He wondered if the man had any other occupation besides ballooning. If not, it seemed like a rather precarious existence. He made a mental note to seek the man out to satisfy his curiosity before this trip was over.

His thoughts were interrupted by the noise of a small box falling over in the far end of the car behind him. He thought he had checked those stacks of freight earlier. But, with the jarring and the constant rocking of the car, something had apparently jiggled loose.

He got up and walked back to the piled boxes and bags. He had to squeeze between some heavy crates and the wall of the car. Just as he emerged into an open space behind, he caught a quick movement out of the corner of his eye. His heart leapt into his throat and his hand was on the butt of his Colt. He stood still, looking carefully around, but saw nothing. Had an animal somehow gotten in here—a rat, maybe? It was entirely possible. The thought that he had been sleeping in a closed car with a big rat sent a shiver up his spine. He pulled his Lightning and stepped softly around the next stack of barrels and boxes. The figure of a man sprang out almost from under his feet. Jay's throat constricted as he leapt back, his gun going off with a roar as he involuntarily squeezed the trigger.

"Don't shoot, mister. I give up!" the man cried, dropping his knife with a clatter and backing away, his hands raised.

Jay recovered quickly from his sudden fright and brought the pistol down level once more, trying to keep his hand from shaking. He was glad his first shot had gone wild into the wall. The weasel-like face of the man opposite him looked vaguely familiar, but he couldn't place it. The man was short, thin and wiry, with a narrow face that was covered with a stubble of black beard. Jay gazed at him for a few moments and neither of them spoke. Now that he had him, what was he to do next?

"Get out from behind there and move up to the other end," Jay finally ordered, his own voice sounding strange. He jabbed his gun in the direction he wanted the man to go. As the slight figure turned his back to obey, Jay stooped quickly to retrieve the dirk the man had dropped and shoved it under his belt.

"Sit there." He motioned to the only chair in the car. The man collapsed into the captain's chair by the desk like a loose sack of bones, and Jay noticed the pinched look of his cheeks, as if he were half-starved. Jay put a foot up on the endboard of the bunk and leaned his elbows on his knee, the Colt still steady.

"Okay, who are you and what are you doing here?"

There was no reply. Fear had been replaced by hopelessness and defeat. The man refused to meet Jay's hard stare. His furtive eyes were darting about, as if looking for some avenue of escape. Then he fixed his gaze above Jay's head at the window. Jay noted the high rock wall of Burning

Rock Cut sliding past the opposite side door window. They were in the Bitter Creek Valley.

"Give me some reason why I shouldn't shoot you," Jay said, having no intention of injuring the intruder, but trying to force a reply.

The man still hesitated to speak. "Gimme a drink o' water," he finally croaked.

Jay went to the water barrel and pumped a tin cup full of water while keeping his eyes on his captive.

The man gulped down the water greedily, slopping some of it down the front of his sack coat in his haste. "More!" he gasped, holding out the cup with both hands.

Jay refilled the cup and the man drained it again. Jay took the cup as the man wiped his mouth with the back of his hand.

Jay waited. The man did not speak so he did.

"This train's moving, we're in the middle of the Wyoming Territory, and this car's locked, so there's no place for you to go. Besides, I'm holding a loaded gun on you, so you'd better start giving me some information."

The stranger nodded his head dejectedly. "I stowed aboard just before the train left Oakland," he muttered.

"Speak up. I can't hear you. Have you been in this car all this time?"

An affirmative nod.

"What's your name?"

"Marvin Cutter."

A flood of recognition broke over Jay as he saw before him the pickpocket Fred Casey had arrested in Golden Gate Park. The thief had escaped jail the night before the train left San Francisco.

"Aren't you a little out of your territory? There's nobody to steal from here, except me . . . and possibly Wells Fargo." He jerked his head toward the safe.

"I just had to get out of the city. And this train seemed like a good way to get as far away as fast as possible." He shrugged, his eyes downcast.

"I doubt if they'd have started a manhunt for a petty thief who managed to escape the city jail. As well as the police know you, they probably figure they could pick you up 'most anytime."

"That's not it." Cutter shook his head averting his gaze.

"What, then? Did you pull off some big robbery just before you jumped the train?"

Again a negative shake of the head. "I can't say."

"Well, no matter. I'll let the law at Rawlings deal with you. We'll be stopping there later this afternoon."

For the first time, Cutter showed some genuine interest.

"What? No. You can't put me off. Please. Not out here in the middle of nowhere. I'd die. There are no people. Please, I can't be marooned in some little whistle-stop town surrounded by Indians."

Jay had to smile. "A city boy, born and reared, I take it? Don't worry, most of the hostile Indians have been run off from around here. I doubt they'll keep you long in Rawlings. More than likely they'll ship you back to San Francisco in handcuffs on the next train west, if the city will pay for a deputy to escort you back. The sheriff at Rawlings will probably send a telegraph message first to find out just what major crime you're wanted there for now."

"Please," Cutter whined, a pitiful look on his lean face, "please don't turn me over to the law until we get to Chicago or Omaha. I won't try to escape. I promise. I even have a few dollars I can give you to buy me some food. I haven't eaten in three days. Besides, I ain't wanted for any crimes, at least not for any big crimes. I just lifted a rich man's wallet so's I'd have a few dollars to get the ferry across to Oakland and out of the city. I gotta be in a town of some size. I'd die out in this godforsaken wilderness."

Jay considered the plea. The man did present a ragged, half-starved appearance, and he almost felt a twinge of pity for the wretched individual. But what was he going to do with him between here and Omaha or Chicago?

"Stand up so I can frisk you."

Cutter stood and held his arms out. Jay went around behind him and patted him down for any concealed weapons. He found none. If he had had a gun, he would have used it to defend himself, instead of the knife, Jay thought. He didn't know what Marvin Cutter had done to be so desperate to get out of his native San Francisco, but that was really no concern of his. His immediate problem was what to do with the man. He was an accomplished thief. Was he also an accomplished liar? Was this fear of being put off in a small town only a ruse? Maybe he had some other reason for wanting to get to Omaha or Chicago. Perhaps he felt his chances better of escaping and disappearing in a large number of people. But would he, Jay, get into trouble for not turning this man over immediately to the conductor or engineer, or at least the next law officer they encountered, probably at the next stop in Rawlings? He might lose his job by harboring a criminal in his car all the way to Chicago. Even if he told the train crew about it, they could do nothing. The only possible place Cutter could be kept a prisoner was in the caboose or right here in the express car. And the caboose was really too small to accommodate another person. Jay made up his mind.

"You'll stay in this car as my prisoner until we get to Omaha, and then I'm turning you over to the law."

There was an almost imperceptible relaxing of tension from the face of Marvin Cutter.

Jay holstered the pistol. Apparently no one had heard his wild shot or the train crew would have been here to check by now. But how was he to keep this man shackled? He wished he had a pair of Fred Casey's handcuffs. But even if he did, there was nothing in the car he could attach him to. He would just have to tie Cutter's hands and feet at night to prevent any opportunity for the thief to attack or kill him in his bunk. While awake, this slippery individual would take a lot of watching.

He reached into a tool box under the shotgun rack and brought out a length of twine.

"Move over to the side door there."

Cutter did as he was told.

"Stretch out your arms."

Cutter stood with his back to the sliding door and held out both arms while Jay cut a piece of the twine with the thief's knife and tied each outstretched arm securely to the metal guides of the sliding door.

"I'm going to get you some food."

He let himself out the end door with his key, relocked it from the outside, and made his way back through the train to the caboose, where he convinced the conductor he was still hungry and begged some of the thick vegetable beef soup the crew kept simmering on the pot-bellied stove. The portly conductor filled an empty lard bucket and capped it for him. Jay tore a generous hunk from a loaf of bread that lay wrapped on a cutting board next to the stove. The round-faced conductor arched his eyebrows at him. "Thought I saw you polish off a steak and potatoes hardly an hour ago in Rock Springs."

"I'm still a growing boy, Tom. I need my nourishment."

The conductor shook his head. "Eating like that, I don't know how you stay so lean."

On impulse, Jay reached into his pocket and fished out a silver dollar and laid it on the cutting board. "Put that in the kitty. And thanks." He took the bucket and bread and went out the door. Thief or not, he was not about to let a man go hungry.

Chapter Five

Cutter was released and sat down, cross-legged, on the floor with the bucket between his legs. Jay thought he had never seen anyone so hungry. Cutter tried to appear that he was not hurrying, but he emptied the soup container and wiped it out with the last of the bread in record time, it seemed to Jay who sat on his bunk, watching. Neither man spoke. When the bucket was empty, Jay retrieved it and rinsed it out at the water barrel, and gave Cutter another drink of water.

Only after several swallows, did Cutter pause, wipe his mouth, and look directly at Jay for a second or two.

"Thanks," he muttered, his gaze skittering away again, like a man who was used to cowering and being kicked. But maybe it was all an act so his captor would relax his guard. After all, Jay reminded himself, this man lived by his cunning.

"Too bad I can't trust you," Jay said with sincere regret. "I'll have to tie you to one of those crates in back at night so I can sleep."

Marvin Cutter nodded, looking at the floor as if he expected nothing better.

"Hate to do it," Jay continued, "but I have no choice. I didn't tell the rest of the crew about you. I don't know why. Anyway, I'll buy you some supper when we stop at Rawlings."

Jay felt the tempo of the train begin to change and he knew exactly where they were. The locomotive was laboring to pull them on the long, gradual upgrade toward Table Rock on the Continental Divide. The noise of the huffing engine reached them through the closed forward door of the car as the speed slowed.

"Drag that chair over next to the wall where I can see you," Jay commanded. He stretched out on his bunk with a magazine. He slipped his pistol out of its holster and laid it on the blanket beside him, ready to hand. As an afterthought he reached into his duffle bag under the bunk and pulled out another magazine.

"Can you read?"

A hurt look came across Cutter's face. Jay flipped the magazine to him. "Here's a copy of the *Police Gazette*." The irony of the title didn't escape him. Cutter caught the magazine in his long, thin hands without changing expression. After a few moments of hesitation, he began leafing through its pages.

But it wasn't long until Marvin Cutter's eyes began to grow heavy and his head to droop. The magazine slipped from his fingers to the floor. Jay took an extra blanket from the foot of his bunk and draped it over the sleeping man. Apparently, the hot food and the relief of tension from his hiding had combined to affect him like a sleeping powder.

Jay sat back down on his bunk and observed the figure slumped in the chair against the wall. He was beginning to have misgivings about trying to keep this man under guard all the way to Omaha.

A sudden jolt of the car nearly threw Jay sideways on his bunk. Steel screeched on steel as the air brakes locked the wheels of the slow-moving train. Couplings banged as the coaches slammed together.

Jay McGraw jumped up and grabbed his pistol from the bunk. What was going on? Probably cattle on the track. It happened often in this unfenced open range. Several had been hit and killed on his own runs. The buffalo were nearly all gone, and the thousands of antelope were wary enough and quick enough to stay well away from the railbed, and the presence of men.

With a glance back at Cutter who had only stirred under his blanket but had not awakened, Jay went to look out the grimy glass of the small, barred window in the forward door. He could see nothing but the back of the tender just ahead and flat areas of sagebrush stretching away out of his vision on either side of the end platform. He took the ring of keys from his belt and let himself out the door. Leaving the door unlocked, he stepped down the three steps on the north side of the train and looked forward. Five horses stood near the engine. Two of them were riderless, and masked men were astride the other three. He turned back and scrambled up, slipping on the metal step and banging his shin. At the same instant he heard a gunshot, and a bullet spanged off the metal step where he had just been standing. Gasping, he fumbled with the key ring for a second or two until he remembered he had left the door unlocked. He leapt inside, slammed the door and quickly locked it, standing to one side, away from the small window.

He raced the length of the car and snatched the shotgun from its rack. His heart pounding and his hands trembling, he broke open the weapon to check the load. He had never been involved in a robbery attempt before and he had often wondered how he would react. Now he knew. He was scared. He snapped the weapon closed, reached into the box under the rack, and grabbed a handful of shells, dropping them into his side coat pocket. Then he remembered he had not reloaded the one shot he had taken from his Colt. Standing the shotgun against the wall, he fumbled in his gunbelt for a fresh cartridge. The shell dropped to the floor. This would never do. He had faced men with guns before. He took a deep breath and exhaled slowly. He concentrated on calming himself. These robbers could be after only one thing—the contents of his safe. It held unknown thousands of dollars worth of greenbacks, gold, and unsigned banknotes. The safety of this express car was his responsibility. It was his sole reason for being here. He took another deep breath, rotated the cylinder of his Colt, punched the empty shell out, and replaced it with a fresh cartridge. He snapped the loading gate shut, lowered the hammer from half-cock, and reholstered the Lightning. Then he took up the shotgun and glanced over at Marvin Cutter. The thin man stirred slightly, pulled the blanket around his shoulders, and slept on. Jay felt a wave of irritation that he should be saddled with this man just now. Whatever was coming, he didn't want to be watching his back. He didn't trust Cutter. Skinny and weak-looking he may have been, but Jay did not underestimate him. For all he knew, Cutter might be a confederate of these robbers, whoever they were. It seemed very coincidental that these gunmen should show up just when he had a petty thief as a stowaway.

But he couldn't worry about that now. He positioned himself behind a large crate and kept his eyes glued on the window in the forward door.

He could hear and see nothing. The slow panting of the locomotive was the only sound. For a long minute, he could hear no other noise. He turned sideways so he could also keep an eye on the sleeping Cutter if, in fact, he *was* still sleeping, and not feigning it until a critical moment.

Jay heard a metallic clinking. He guessed the engine was being uncoupled from the train. A muffled voice sounded somewhere, but he couldn't make out the words. Jay saw the brakeman's head move past the window. A few seconds later he heard the locomotive's deep-throated roar as the back of the tender began to pull away. He sprang up to the door, holding the shotgun ready, and flattened himself alongside the window. He carefully peered out through the grimy glass between the closely spaced bars. The engine continued to pull away and Jay saw the three horsemen, still mounted, one of them holding the horses of the two he presumed were in the cab of the locomotive. Less than a quarter-mile ahead, the engine puffed across a small wooden trestle and continued on for another several hundred yards before coming to a halt. A figure dropped down from the engine and ran back to the trestle. A few seconds later, he raced back toward the engine, running with a strange, bowlegged stride. Just as the man reached the tender, the wooden trestle erupted in a mushroom of splintered timbers, smoke, dust and flame. Twisted rails and pieces of wood rained down into the dry wash for several seconds as the sound of the blast faded on the wind.

Jay swallowed hard. His mouth was dry. The train was being isolated from the locomotive. The head of the snake was being cut off. These men were serious and obviously well prepared.

Maybe he could muster some firepower to resist them. The engineer and stoker were already in the hands of the attackers. Very likely the brakeman as well. The conductor might still be free in the rear of the train, but he did not carry a gun, not even a pocket pistol. The passengers were an unknown quantity. They looked to be a mixed group with several women and even three or four small children among them.

On a sudden impulse, he ran to the rear door, let himself out and crossed the adjoining platforms to the first passenger coach in one quick bound.

"We're under attack!" he yelled to the full coach. A woman stifled a scream, and the coach erupted in a clamor of excited talk. Everyone was crowding the windows.

"What was that explosion?" one man asked.

"They unhitched the engine and pulled it across the bridge and then dynamited the bridge. We're isolated. Any of you men who are armed and want to help defend this train, get up to the express car—quick!"

Three men got up and started forward.

Jay ran down the aisle toward the next car.

He shouted his message in the second car and got two recruits. He sent one of them to the Pullman and caboose to spread the word.

He dared waste no more time. He had taken only a couple of minutes, but it may have been too much.

Six men were crowded at the door of the first passenger coach, waiting for him. Just as he reached them, a gun boomed outside and glass exploded somewhere ahead. The men turned to stare at him. One wore the blue coat and yellow leg stripes of a cavalry officer. Another was in buckskin. A third sported muttonchop sidewhiskers under a bowler hat. And, to Jay's surprise, there stood Fletcher Hall, the aeronaut.

"The express car's locked," buckskin said, peering out the door. "One of 'em just put a slug through the side window."

Jay ground his teeth. They were trapped outside the express car.

"Open that door, and do it quick!" came the yell from one of the robbers who remained out of their line of sight. Jay squeezed past the men and opened the door a crack. He could see two of the mounted horsemen. Jay suddenly remembered Marvin Cutter. The thief must be cowering in the corner if he was awakened by a shot and a shower of glass. Should he even try to slip back inside the locked car with a couple of men? Even if he made it, they could not see out to shoot. He wished there were some sort of loopholes in the walls of the car. It was poorly designed for an active defense. You had to stay inside and lock the enemy out, similar to the way a terrapin defends itself.

"C'mon outa that car! If you don't open that door, we'll blast you out!" came the shout. "You have two minutes—starting now!"

Jay had to make a quick decision. He couldn't let them get away with the cash without a fight. He slipped out the door and thrust his head around the right side of the train. No one there. Good. They were all on the north side of the train just as he had guessed. He ducked back inside, and made a quick survey of the six men who were still crowded by the door.

"Lieutenant, Hall, and you," he pointed at the man in buckskin. "Come with me. The rest of you stay here and be ready to start shooting when you hear us fire."

He carefully opened the door again and led them down the steps of the platform. "They're all on the north side," he whispered. "Get to the other end and get them in a crossfire before they have a chance to use that dynamite."

The four men ran, single-file, down the uneven roadbed, the north wind whipping puffs of dust from under their boots.

"Hey! There's somebody on the other side!" one of the attackers shouted. A gun boomed and a lead slug whined off an iron rail just in front of Jay. Someone tripped and fell behind him. Jay dropped to his belly and took a quick look underneath at the horsemen. Two of them were spurring their horses toward the end of the car to come around after them. Jay was still a dozen feet from the end of the express car, but he sprang up to one knee, cocked both barrels of his shotgun and waited. As the first horse vaulted the tracks and came into view, he let go the first barrel. It was a clean miss, but the rider let out a wild yell of surprise and was nearly pitched headlong as his horse stumbled on the uneven ground. Jay touched off the second shot before the bandit could recover his balance. A few of the pellets stung the bay's rump. The animal squealed in pain and went racing back across the tracks and out of view.

Jay glanced back and saw the cavalry officer standing just behind him with his long-barrelled Army Colt in hand. The buckskin man and Fletcher Hall were flat on their bellies, firing at the attackers from under the tall express car. Jay and the lieutenant ran to the end and, crouching behind the iron platform, began firing at the five riders who had backed about thirty yards away from the car. Their horses were dancing and plunging as the gunmen were having trouble returning fire. The attackers had lost the initiative, and the raid was stalling.

One of the riders yelled suddenly and grabbed his leg. As his horse spun, Jay could see a red stain spreading on his thigh. Jay could tell by the sound of the shots that the other three men who had remained in the passenger coach were getting in their share.

Finally, on a signal from their leader, the five would-be robbers pulled their horses around and galloped off through the gray-green sage. He heard a cheer go up from the men at the far end.

Jay stood up, becoming aware of how tense he was. In spite of the chill wind, he was sweating. He flipped open the loading gate of his Colt Lightning and began punching out the empties. He set the shotgun on the ground to reload next.

"That was just the first round," the soldier behind him said. Jay turned and, for the first time, took a good look at the man instead of just at the blue uniform. What he saw was a hatless young man of about his own height with blond hair and a mustache. He had a frank, open face that was slightly windburned.

"John Ormand," he said, shifting his gun to his left and extending his right hand.

"Jay McGraw. Thanks for your help, Lieutenant." They shook hands. "I'm afraid you're right," Jay continued, trying to calm the shaky reaction that was beginning to set in, now that the adrenalin was beginning to ebb. Maybe if he were under fire every day, or even once a month, he might get used to it, but he was certainly having trouble keeping his hands and voice from shaking now.

All seven men came out from their hiding places and gathered on the north side of the express car as the retreating bandits disappeared over a rise in the grass and sage a half-mile away.

The man in the bowler hat and sideburns was mopping his brow with a handkerchief. They introduced themselves all around. The man with the bowler hat was a whiskey drummer named Clyde McFee. In addition to Fletcher Hall, the aeronaut, and John Ormand, the Second Lieutenant returning to Fort Laramie from leave, the lean man in the greasy buckskins was Jim Donovan, a hunter who attempted to keep Fort Laramie supplied with fresh meat during the winter. The other two were Ambrose Skelton, a topographical engineer with the U.S. Geological Survey, and Roger Decker, a balding, well-dressed storekeeper from North Platte, Nebraska.

Decker and Skelton went back to calm and reassure the passengers while Jay, temporarily forgetting about his unwelcome guest, unlocked the door and let the rest of them into the express car to hold a council of war.

As soon as he walked in, he remembered, but it was too late as the rest of them crowded in behind him to get out of the cold wind. Cutter was nowhere in sight. Jay glanced sharply around, but there was no sign of him. He was relieved that the thief had had the good sense to get out of sight somewhere behind the freight. The floor was strewn with broken glass. The five men sat on the bunk or leaned against the desk, and one sat in the only chair. A few seconds of silence followed as the four looked expectantly at Jay.

"We're isolated here," Jay began, standing in front of them. "The loco-motive is on the other side of that dynamited bridge."

"They made the engineer pull away at least a quarter-mile," Donovan, the hunter, said.

"He might as well keep goin' to Rawlings for help, cause he can't get back to hook up to us," Lieutenant Ormand said.

"What do we do now?" Donovan asked.

"Anybody got any suggestions?" Jay asked, breaking open his shotgun and popping out the empty casings. He reloaded from the shells he carried in his coat pocket.

"They'll be back, that's for sure," Fletcher Hall said.

"You're right," Jay said. "So we'd better make some plans, fast."

"At least one of them's shot in the leg," Donovan remarked. "Might be they'll stay away awhile and lick their wounds."

"Maybe, but I doubt it. The longer they wait, the sooner somebody will miss this train and send a relief."

"How long 'til dark?"

"Probably three hours, give or take," Lieutenant Ormand replied. "Days are getting shorter, and with these dark clouds . . ." He shrugged.

"If they don't come back in the next twenty minutes, I'm betting they'll wait and make a night attack," Jay said, hoping he sounded convincing. "If I were out there trying to pull off this robbery, that's what I'd do. I'd slip up here after dark when the defenders can't see to shoot, throw a couple of sticks of dynamite under this car or through the window, then blow the safe and ride off in the dark."

"Not a chance," the aeronaut said, shaking his head. "In the first place, people who rob trains get nervous. They'd burn three hours of daylight if they did it your way—three hours when they could be putting distance between themselves and any pursuit."

Jay experienced a flush of anger at the pontificating of this pompous ass. The man delivered his opinion as if he were lecturing to a crowd of dimwits. Jay could feel his face reddening. "What do *you* think they'll do?" he asked, trying to keep his voice casual.

Before he could answer, the door opened and the engineer came in, dabbing at a bruise on his forehead with a red bandanna. "Boys, I'd a' been gone a good ways to Rawlings by now, but they blew a hole in my boiler."

"Damn! Where's your stoker?" Jay asked, glancing around.

"Charley's hurt bad. He went for one of 'em with a shovel when they jumped us, but they laid him out with a wrench. He hasn't made a sound since. He's breathin', but I think his skull's busted. He may not make it.

The brakeman's up yonder lookin' after him. Didn't think we oughta try movin' him just now. They threatened to shoot me if I didn't do exactly as they said. Made me run the engine up the track a ways, and then disabled the boiler and some o' the lines so she won't hold no steam. I heard all the shootin' while I was walkin' back here."

"We're stuck here, then," Donovan said. "Any chance a relief train might come lookin' for us any time soon?"

The engineer shook his head. "They'll know we're overdue right quick. The telegraph wire has been cut. But it'll be a few hours before we see anyone come looking."

"Any chance they'll send a posse on horseback instead of a train?" Lieutenant Ormand asked.

The engineer shrugged, pumping himself a drink of water from the barrel in the corner. "Dunno. Maybe. But they don't know we're being attacked. They probably think we jumped the track or broke down. 'Course that wire bein' cut may give 'em a clue. All I know is that engine ain't goin' nowhere on its own until the boiler's fixed in a machine shop."

"Well, we'd better see to the defense of this train for however long we're going to be here," the lieutenant said. "Maybe, since the passengers have seen that we drove these bandits off once, we can get some more recruits among the men to help us do it again if we have to."

"Oh, we'll have to, all right," Fletcher Hall stated. "And soon."

"How much ammunition have we got if we have to stand off a seige?" Jay asked of the assembly.

The men looked at one another and began checking the cartridge loops in their belts. There were no rifles among them.

The door opened and Roger Decker, the storekeeper, burst in. "Here they come again!"

Chapter Six

The second attempt to rob the express car was beaten off a little easier than the first but only because Jay McGraw and his men were more prepared.

One of the four raiders was able to ride close enough to hurl a sputtering bundle of dynamite sticks at the express car before he caught a bullet in the shoulder and galloped away, reeling on his horse and clinging to the saddle horn. The dynamite stick bounced under the coupling between the Wells Fargo car and the first passenger coach and exploded. The men crouching behind the platform saw it coming in time to run about forty yards back into the sage before the fuse touched off the blast. It snapped the coupling and derailed the express car, lifting one end and setting its wheel truck just off the rails. The glass in several of the coach windows was blown out. Except for a few of the passengers getting minor cuts from flying glass, no one was hurt, while the man who threw the dynamite had been put out of action by a disabling, and possibly fatal, bullet wound.

Jay McGraw had been firing from behind the forward wheel truck when the dynamite was thrown and had time only to run a few steps and throw himself flat on his stomach before the blast.

Following the explosion that splintered the floor and twisted the iron platform at one end of the express car, one of the three remaining bandits made a rush and managed to reach the car while all the defenders were gone.

As Jay scrambled to his feet, his ears still ringing, he saw a figure leap from his horse to the twisted metal of the platform. He kicked open the door and disappeared inside. Jay, his head still spinning and ears ringing from the concussion, staggered toward the car. Lieutenant Ormand and Donovan had seen the bandit get inside also. The man would have to come out somewhere—perhaps by opening one of the big side doors. He could not blow the safe while he was still in there. They had to stop him before he could set a charge. Jay counted only four raiders this time. They had left the wounded man behind somewhere. And now the dynamite thrower had been wounded. That left only three. Surely they could drive off three attackers with seven guns.

Lieutenant Ormand was the first one to reach the broken end door. Through a blur of blowing dust, Jay saw him go in. The firing had commenced again, the defenders exchanging shots with the two horsemen who were cavorting on the other side of the train. Donovan, Hall, and Jay all reached the wrecked end of the car at the same time. The officer had not come out. Jay crept up and jumped inside the shattered door, Colt ready. Lieutenant Ormand was diving across the glass-littered floor. He grabbed a sputtering stick of dynamite next to the safe and, in the same fluid motion, rolled and flung it out the side door the robber had slid open.

Jay instinctively dropped behind the corner of the roll-top desk and, in the space of three heartbeats, another terrific explosion rocked the car. Dirt and sand showered through the open doorway. Lieutenant Ormand rolled up to his hands and knees, his head hanging down.

Jay sprang to the edge of the open doorway just in time to see three raiders galloping away again. He lowered his Colt and let out a long breath, his heart pounding. He was suddenly aware, as the cold wind struck him, that he was sweating. He wiped a hand across the moisture on his forehead, and his fingers came away mixed with blood. He had been struck by a piece of flying glass or gravel and had a slight, stinging cut near his hairline. He turned to look after Lieutenant Ormand who was sitting on the floor, a fingertip to one ear.

"Damn near deafened me," he said, speaking louder than necessary. Donovan and Hall entered the car.

"Well, they're gone again, but probably not for long," the auburn-haired Hall remarked, barely glancing at the officer. His manner was cocksure.

Hardly a wavy auburn hair on his head was out of place, Jay noted. He was not sweaty and dirty as the rest of them were. As he spoke, he was automatically reloading his storekeeper's model Colt .45.

The man was a boor, Jay thought, complimenting himself that his first impression of the man had been right. If Hall remembered their meeting at the reception in San Francisco, he gave no indication of it.

Jay walked to the partially open side door and looked out again. The bold raider who had entered the car and planted the burning dynamite stick at the safe apparently had had his horse brought up to the door by one of his friends so he could make a quick getaway. Jay could see the three of them now, sitting their horses just out of range, watching the train. The defenders had reduced the number of attackers to three. Jay wondered idly where the two wounded men were. Were they dying? Had they been able to ride somewhere to safety where they'd be cared for by their friends? As he remembered, they had leg and shoulder wounds which were probably not fatal, unless the bullets had cut an artery somewhere.

He turned away from the door and glanced around on the floor for his cap. It was gone and he had no idea where. He was suddenly terribly weary. Lieutenant Ormand had regained his feet as the other defenders began to drift in, picking their way around the splintered floorboards near the end door.

Jay made his way past them as they grinned and congratulated each other on having driven off the robbers a second time. He could hear the confidence level rising in their voices. But this second victory had been costly, Jay discovered as he entered the first passenger coach. Ambrose Skelton, the topographical engineer, had been struck in the head by a bullet. He was still breathing, but unconscious.

"No doctor aboard," Clyde McFee, the short whiskey drummer, told Jay as he came up. "And, even if there was, I doubt he could do anything for the poor devil. I think it's only a matter of time. And a short time, at that." McFee laid his bowler hat aside on the upholstered seat and unbuttoned his vest to breathe easier. The unconscious man was stretched out in the aisle, face down, and had been covered with a blanket. His coat had been rolled up for a pillow. His breathing was ragged.

"Anybody else hurt?" Jay asked.

"Nope. Lot of people were scared though." He nodded toward the rest of the passengers. Several pale faces were cautiously peering out from under the seats and looking out the shattered windows to see if the battle was over. A young mother was trying to soothe the whimpering of a little girl about three years old.

Jay glanced out the window. The three raiders had now disappeared entirely. He wondered if they were gone for good, or had just retreated to regroup and plan the strategy of their next attack. He could only guess. Maybe the wounding of two of their number would be enough to discourage them from any further attempts. They probably had not expected the organized resistance they had met. On the other hand, they had effectively crippled the train and the treasure was there for the taking, if they could somehow quickly destroy the resistance that Jay had mustered on the spur of the moment.

Jay stepped around the wounded man and went to the next coach where he found the conductor passing out coffee he had brewed in the large pot in the caboose and trying to reassure the passengers that everything was going to be all right. His bland, round face and calm manner seemed to be having the desired effect on some of them. Jay wished he felt as confident as he nodded to the portly, black-coated man. He ignored the questioning look in the conductor's eyes and made his way back toward the front of the train. He stepped out onto the end platform of the passenger coach where the engineer and the four defenders, excluding McFee and the wounded man, were standing or sitting on the steps, holding another council of war.

As Jay pushed aside the shattered door, a swirling gust of cold wind whipped fine sand against the side of his face and forced all of them to shield their faces from the stinging blast.

"Think they're coming back, McGraw?" Lieutenant Ormand asked.

"Depends on how badly they want that treasure," Jay replied. "Personally, if it were me out there, and I was well supplied with dynamite, and I had gone to all this trouble already, you can bet I'd give it at least one more good try before anyone had time to come looking for us. As of right now, they have absolutely nothing to show for their efforts except two wounded men."

"Yeah, but maybe they want to live to fight another day. Maybe rob a stage or something that's easier pickin's," Buckskin Donovan said.

"I suppose it depends on how determined they are. We stung their pride. They might want to get us now, no matter what the cost."

Fletcher Hall, the aeronaut, had not spoken. He was leaning his buttocks against the twisted iron railing of the platform, his arms folded across his chest, listening to the conversation.

"Why don't we just give 'em the money?" the engineer asked, spitting between his knees into the sand from where he sat on the upper step.

No one spoke for a few moments. This alternative, Jay thought, had probably not even occurred to these men. They were all fighters, including the self-assured aeronaut. The silence lengthened, broken only by the whistling of the wind through the brush. The engineer apparently took this as a unanimous negative because he said no more.

"What do we do now?" Donovan, the lean hunter asked. "I'm completely out of ammunition. Didn't think I would need my Winchester this trip, so I left it at the fort."

"I'm down to six shots myself," Lieutenant Ormand said.

"Three here," Roger Decker, the storekeeper, said.

"Anybody here carry a .38?" Jay asked. "I've got a good two-hundred rounds left in there." He jerked his head toward the damaged express car. "And there are plenty of shells for the shotgun."

Nobody did. The closest thing was a .41 caliber Derringer that McFee carried in his vest pocket. He had come out the door to join them during the conversation.

Just then the portly conductor opened the door and squeezed outside. He glanced around at the tense faces, his blue eyes wide. "Gentlemen, if they come again, I suggest we give them whatever they want. If they are well armed, we can't expect to hold them off indefinitely and . . ."

"What's this 'we' business?" Hall growled, speaking for the first time. "I don't remember seeing you out here with a gun in your hands."

The conductor's pale, round face flushed pink. "What I mean to say is, I have the responsibility of these passengers. Already one of our number has been shot in the head and is probably dying." He turned toward Jay. "Surely Wells Fargo cannot expect you to defend that express box at the cost of human lives, not to mention railroad property that's worth even more than is probably in your safe."

"We've come this far; there's no giving up now," Jay answered shortly.

"Why don't we take the contents of your safe and bury it out here in the desert before they come back?" Decker suggested.

"Wouldn't work," Jay answered, shaking his head. "If they come again, they're going to be mad and doubly determined. If they get control of this train and find the safe empty, they'll know we hid it someplace, so they'll just threaten or torture some of us until we tell them where it is. I think the safest place for that cash and gold is right where it is. Even if they overpower us, they'll have to blast it open to get at it. I don't know if all of them are experts at handling explosives, but the man who threw the charge under the car was wounded."

"The man who put the dynamite stick by the safe wasn't," Lieutenant Ormand said.

"Look!" The engineer who was sitting on the step was pointing north. Seven riders sat their mounts about a mile away. They all fell silent, straining to see if the robbers were about to make another attack. At this distance, only their hats and clothing identified them as white men. If they were the raiders, they had four more men with them.

"That's the same bunch, right enough. I recognize that Appaloosa on the end," Donovan said.

"We may be in for it now," Jay said, slipping his Lightning out and checking its load.

For a full two minutes they watched the distant horsemen and nobody moved. A faint cry from inside the coach told them that one of the women had also spotted them. The men on the outside platform stared out across the sage- and grass-covered valley. Then the horsemen were gone as quickly as they had come. They wheeled their horses and disappeared over the undulating ground without a sound. Jay rubbed his irritated eyes and looked again at the spot where the images had merged with the gray-green of the vegetation and the dark, overcast, windy sky.

"Just checking us out. And they've got more help this time," the lieutenant observed. "We'd better decide how we're going to handle this."

No one spoke for a long time as they all were either trying to formulate some plan of defense, or were waiting for someone else to come up with a suggestion that would be practical in light of the fact that all but Jay were nearly out of ammunition.

Jay glanced at the sky. He estimated it was probably two hours until sunset. An idea was taking shape in his mind. If it worked, it could save the treasure and any further danger to the rest of the people here. He turned to Fletcher Hall. "How long would it take you to get your gas balloon unpacked and inflated?"

Chapter Seven

"What?"

For the first time, Jay saw a startled look in the aeronaut's blue eyes. But he quickly recovered. "What has my balloon got to do with this?"

"If you can get it into the air, it would be a quick escape for us where they can't follow. You and I could get this treasure box safely away from here and save anyone else from getting hurt at the same time."

Hall shook his head firmly. "Out of the question. The way the wind is blowing, I doubt that we could even keep it under control long enough to inflate and get airborne. Besides, it would take too long to set up all the paraphernalia to generate the gas."

"Why not try? What other choice do we have?" Jay insisted.

"Look," Hall said, as if trying to calm himself enough to explain something to a dim-witted child. "After the acid is sealed in the tank, iron filings have to be added slowly as the gas forms and is pumped into the envelope. It's a complicated procedure that takes several hours. One doesn't just pump up the balloon and take off in a matter of a few minutes. Our friends out there could attack and overwhelm this train and be gone with the loot long before we could even get the wagons unloaded and set up to generate."

"If they were going to attack, why didn't they do it a few minutes ago?"

Donovan wondered aloud. "They must not know we're almost out of ammunition."

"My guess is they're waiting for dark," Jay said. "Even if it cuts down on the time they have to get a head start on the law, they now have reinforcements and, with dynamite and the cover of darkness, they'd have a much better chance. Then, they'd also have the rest of the night to get a long head start on any trackers."

There was a glum silence. The men were staring at their boots or off into the distance, lost in their own thoughts.

"I think we oughta give the balloon idea a try," Donovan finally said. There were several grunts and nods of agreement. "After all, what have we got to lose?"

"It will cost me several hundred dollars to get that balloon into the air, and maybe several thousands of dollars if it's wrecked," Fletcher Hall replied sharply.

"I'm sure Wells Fargo or the railroad will reimburse you for any losses," Jay said, trying to keep his voice even and convincing. He really had no assurance that this was true.

"Yeah, I've seen how fast some of these companies pay up after the danger is past," Hall replied sarcastically. "About as fast as the government does. No, you can forget about using my balloon. It would never work."

"Mr. Hall," Lieutenant Ormand said, turning to face him and drawing his Colt. "I am declaring this an emergency. As an officer in the U.S. Army, I'm sworn to protect the citizens of this country. In this situation, I feel it's my duty to commandeer your balloon and equipment. It's probably our only chance of escaping these outlaws without further loss of life." In spite of his youthful appearance, there was no mistaking the steel in his voice.

"You can't do that. You have no authority!" The aeronaut's eyes bugged slightly and the veins swelled in his neck.

"Oh, yes I do. Don't make me have to enforce my order."

Hall's face reddened, but he glanced quickly around at the assemblage of grim faces and apparently decided that he'd try to save what face he could.

"All right. But I have witnesses that I was forced into this. It'll never work, I tell you!"

"Shut up and show us how to get your stuff unloaded," Donovan said.

Hall glared at him.

38

"It's in two wagons back on the flatcar," Hall said finally, his voice dropping in resignation.

All seven of them, including the engineer, dropped off both sides of the platform and ran back along the sides of the train toward the flatcar that was just behind the Pullman and just ahead of the caboose.

While the engineer stood watch for another attack, the others swarmed over the two wagons, unlashing the heavy covers.

"Be careful of that! Set it down over here. Carefully!" The corner of a wooden crate slipped out of Decker's hands and the box was yanked out of Donovan's grasp on the other end, falling two feet to the platform with a crash.

"You clumsy idiots!" Hall screamed.

The buckskin-clad hunter gave the raving Hall a hard look, started to say something, then bit it off and leaned down with Decker to retrieve the crate.

Hall paced up and down alongside the train, red-faced, giving orders and directing movements of the gear that was being unloaded. At last came the balloon itself, enclosed in its netting of cord.

"Keep those lines straight when you unroll that!" Fletcher Hall was yelling. "If they get tangled, we'll never get them straightened out."

Jay and the rest of the men unfolded and unrolled the big envelope and stretched it out on the ground along the right-of-way on the southern, downwind, side of the flatcar.

"Don't snag it on those bushes," Hall was yelling.

The men were working quickly, but carefully, as if aware that, obnoxious as he was, Fletcher Hall was the only one who knew anything about this balloon and thus might be their only hope of escape from the next onslaught of the train robbers.

Finally, the balloon was spread out to his satisfaction, and the supporting lines all pulled straight to the wicker basket that lay on its side. Hall then directed the lining up of the containers for the carboys of hydrochloric acid, the wooden kegs of iron filings, and the pump that would draw off the hydrogen gas formed by the combining of the acid and the iron. The pump was connected to a hose that fastened to the base of the cambric envelope. Hall had told them it would be a long, laborious process. The iron filings had to be slowly added to the acid, the gas generated and then worked by the hand pump into the huge balloon. It was nearly a half-hour before everything was ready and the first iron filings were being added under Hall's watchful eye. Jay began to realize how long this procedure was going to take. Hall had not been exaggerating.

Jay glanced at the sky. The wind was still blowing, but the low clouds were shredding and blowing away to the southeast. The late afternoon sun was throwing intermittent shafts of light across the gray-green sage of the high desert valley. He looked off to the north where the raiders had disappeared. How much longer would they give the besieged train? He hoped his theory was correct. He assumed that they were waiting to attack under the cover of darkness. It was almost too much to hope that the robbers had given up for good.

Jay climbed back up onto the flatcar and leaned on one of the two wagons, staring off to the north where the robbers had been last seen. He nervously loosened the Colt in its holster, hardly aware he was doing it. As he leaned over the edge of the heavy Studebaker wagon, his arm bumped something hard. He threw back the corner of the loose canvas cover. It was the metal valve atop a cylindrical metal tank. He pulled the cover all the way off and saw a dozen of these tanks held in a wooden rack just inside the sideboard of the wagon. He stepped up on the wheel hub and into the wagon for a closer look. But there were no markings on the canisters that he could see. Another dozen rested in a row on the opposite side of the wagon. He tried lifting one of the tanks. It weighed a good seventy or eighty pounds. He let the cylinder slide back into place.

Fletcher Hall looked up sharply when he heard the sound it made.

"Hey! Leave your hands off those tanks!" he yelled at Jay. The other men looked up to see what he was riled about.

"Get out of that wagon!" Hall said, hopping up onto the flatcar.

"What are these?" Jay asked, making no move to climb out.

"None o' your damn business. That's my property. Now, get outa there."

"They look like some sort of pressure tanks," Jay continued, a little taken aback at this volatile reaction. He had a sudden, uncontrollable urge to needle this man, more than he did to find out what the tanks contained.

"I said, get away from those tanks!" Hall was leaning over the tailgate of the wagon, his face beet-red.

"I only wanted to know what was in 'em," Jay said with feigned innocence.

Hall looked around, suddenly aware of the attention he was drawing. The men who were adding the iron filings to the acid had stopped and were staring at him. Even several of the passengers from the Pullman had come outside to see what the shouting was all about. He lowered his voice, and tried, unsuccessfully, to assume a casual attitude. "They're just dangerous, that's all. They contain compressed gas. You don't want to bump those valves on top. They could explode. Very dangerous," he muttered, sidling away from the wagon, but keeping an eye on Jay McGraw, who hadn't moved. "They're experimental. Don't want to jar them around. That's why I built those special racks to carry them," he added, lamely.

"What do they have to do with ballooning?" Jay persisted.

Hall glanced sharply at him and then around to see if the others were listening. "Nothing, really," he said, trying to pass the matter off. "They contain compressed hydrogen. The British Army has been trying to devise a method of carrying gas into the field for their balloon corps in Africa, and this is finally what they came up with. They've been experimenting with it for several years, but they've had trouble devising a valve that was gas-tight. These are the latest efforts. They think they've finally got it perfected."

"Have you used them?" Jay asked.

"Once before."

"Did they work?"

Hall plainly wanted to drop the subject, but he finally answered. "Yes."

"What's the advantage over this method?" Jay pressed, leaning on the wooden rack and nodding at the gas-generating procedure going on below him.

"Not as much equipment to haul around. Fewer people needed to get the balloon filled."

"Appears to me it'd be a lot quicker, too," Jay said, forcing the obvious. "Yes."

"How much quicker?" he insisted.

Hall looked pained, but trapped. "If we used most of those tanks, we could fill the balloon in less than thirty minutes."

Lieutenant Ormand looked around, startled. "Thirty minutes? Then, what the hell are we doing this for?" He gestured at the gear spread out on the ground.

"Lieutenant, these are still experimental. These could blow up and kill somebody if not handled with extreme care," Hall said.

"Damn the danger! You know how to handle them. Get 'em out here and let's get this thing inflated!" The officer was plainly very irritated.

"I'm saving them for an emergency. They're very expensive and hard to get. I have a friend in a British Army supply unit who . . ."

"Get 'em unloaded!" Lieutenant Ormand interrupted him, drawing his pistol to emphasize his order. "We've already lost enough time. Another word out of you and I'll arrest you for being a part of this gang of robbers."

In less than ten minutes the gas-generating equipment had been dismantled and piled, haphazardly, into the wagons, and the metal cylinders hauled out and handed down. Hall, realizing he was outnumbered and outgunned, threw himself into the task of hooking the valves of each cylinder, in turn, to a special connection at the mouth of the balloon and began discharging his precious cargo of compressed hydrogen into the envelope.

The cambric fabric of the balloon itself was a closely woven linen, sealed and reinforced with a special varnish. At first, the gas seemed to make no appreciable difference in the shape of the envelope as tank after tank of gas was expended into it. Jay eyed the remaining tanks, wondering if there would be enough to fill it. But then the fabric began to lift and swell. Each successive tank formed the cambric into a larger and larger teardrop shape, pushing the material out against the cord netting that enclosed it. Finally, the huge balloon swung clear of the ground and immediately the wind swung it around to the south.

"Keep a grip on it!" Hall yelled as the force of the shifting monster dragged two men across the ground at the end of the ropes they were holding. "Secure those mooring lines to the side of the flatcar," Hall directed, running to assist Donovan and one of the male passengers who had come outside to help. Most of the others had migrated from the cars to watch the operation. It had been almost an hour since the raiders had last appeared and a feeling of confidence and safety seemed to be spreading. Jay and the others who were hurrying to fill the balloon knew better. Time was precious and they had to make the most of it. They could almost be ready to fly now if it hadn't been for the stubbornness of the aeronaut. Jay couldn't account for it. The man stood to lose some money and the hard-to-get and expensive compressed gas, but the people on the train stood to lose a lot more, including their lives, if they continued to resist the attackers. Maybe Fletcher Hall was willing to give up the contents of the express car to the bandits, as the treasure box meant no loss to him. But why had he joined in the defense of the train? He had volunteered to fight. Jay shook his head and looked away at the sky. The man was an enigma. Jay suspected the redhead had fought only so he would not be labeled a coward by any of the others. After all, he was the daredevil aeronaut. He couldn't let his public image suffer.

The balloon was taking on a definite shape now. It was completely clear of the ground and was jerking and tugging at its mooring lines. The wicker basket was securely moored to the edge of the flatcar.

"Better get that treasure box; it won't be long now," Hall said, calmly. Jay looked sideways at him. The man gave no indication that he had been ranting and raving like a maniac only a few minutes earlier. He was now the disciplined professional.

Jay took a quick, admiring look at the billowing shape. The varnished linen was dust-colored, but the cord netting couldn't obscure the magnificent bald eagle that had been painted on the surface of the balloon, its wings spread in full flight.

He hurried back toward the wrecked express car to transfer the cash and bonds from the safe to the green express box. As he knelt alone on the glass-littered floor by the safe and spun the combination dial, his stomach began to tense at the thought of actually flying into the sky in that balloon. Hall had said the wind was too strong to fly. But Jay dismissed this. The aeronaut had made other claims and statements that had proved to be false. If it was unsafe, he wouldn't be flying it himself. But then, hadn't Lieutenant Ormand forced him at gunpoint to make the balloon ready to fly? He swallowed hard. There was no other way out. If the treasure box went, he had to go with it. He found himself almost wishing the robbers had gotten away with it on their first attempt. At least that would have relieved him of the terrifying thought of this balloon flight. He had been to the top of an eight-story hotel once, and had viewed the city from its dizzying height, but he had still felt the solid building under his feet. This time, if they weren't dragged across the desert and smashed against the rocky ground, they would be soaring at the mercy of a gusty wind thousands of feet in the air, with nothing but the gaseous envelope and the thin wicker basket to buoy them up from certain death. Jay closed his eyes and tried to shut out the mental image. The guns of the robbers that he had already faced twice seemed infinitely preferable.

He scooped the contents of the safe into the wooden Wells Fargo box, shut the lid, and snapped the big padlock in place, dropping the key into his pants pocket. Then, as an afterthought, he went to the box under the shotgun rack and picked up two boxes of .38 cartridges for his Colt Lightning and put them into the Wells Fargo box.

Only then did he suddenly remember Marvin Cutter. With a start, he jumped up and looked around. He hadn't thought of the thief since the last attack. He had completely forgotten about the man in all the excitement and confusion. Where was he? Jay squeezed behind the freight boxes and searched the car quickly. There was no sign of him. He had either taken off into the desert and escaped or he was hiding somewhere on or near the train. Except for the knife that Jay had confiscated, Cutter had not been armed. Jay had had the shotgun, so there was no chance he could have armed himself. He stood for a moment in the middle of the floor, pondering what to do. He had more important things to do just now than to organize a search for a man nobody else had seen. Forget him. As long as he stayed out of sight, good riddance.

Jay hoisted the heavy box by its handle on one end. He set it down and, squatting, gripped it by both leather handles on the ends, and lifted.

A rifle shot exploded somewhere. Then a fusillade of shots followed. Jay glanced out the partially opened side door. His stomach knotted as his worst fears were realized. The raiders were galloping toward the train, firing as they came. He was trapped with the treasure box before they could get the balloon airborne.

Chapter Eight

Jay experienced panic as he debated whether he should unlock the box and throw its contents back into the safe. He took another quick look. There were the same seven riders and they were coming at a steady gallop but still a good distance away. He thought maybe he could make it to the balloon. He staggered to the ruined end door with the heavy box and tumbled it off onto the side away from the raiders. Moving as fast as he could, he climbed over the twisted metal of the platform and dropped lightly to the ground beside the box.

As he wrestled the box into his grip again, he saw Buckskin Donovan running toward him alongside the train. Without a word, the lean hunter grabbed the handle on one end of the box while Jay grabbed the other, and the two of them were able to go at a stumbling half-run with their burden. Even so, the inflated balloon seemed a long way off, and Jay heard the shots getting ever closer. He was dimly aware of the cries of the passengers as they fled back into the coaches.

The defenders were crouched behind the cover of the flatcar and the two wagons atop it. But they were not returning fire. What few cartridges that remained among them were apparently being saved for a last-ditch effort.

The balloon was stretched tight inside its cord netting and bulked huge above the train, the painted eagle glaring fiercely down at the humans below. The wind was tugging at the flying machine that was tethered short by two manila lines. The wicker basket rode a bare two feet above the edge of the flatcar.

Hoofbeats and shots were getting closer. They were coming with an all-out assault this time. Jay had no doubt the raiders were laying down a covering fire until they got close enough to dynamite the defenders into submission.

He ducked instinctively as a slug shattered a coach window above him. His feet were slipping and sliding in the slope of soft, sandy soil along the roadbed. The box bumped awkwardly against his legs as he and Donovan tried to keep up a crouching run. The grip was cutting into his fingers and his back was aching from stooping. He was breathing hard.

He glanced up and saw Fletcher Hall holster his gun and come running to help. But he got in the way more than he helped. They hoisted the box up onto the flatcar and then jumped up and heaved it up and over the lip of the gondola.

"Let's move!" Hall said, urgently, peering around one of the wagons. The horsemen were only about fifty yards away now, but Lieutenant Ormand was still having the men hold their fire.

Hall cupped his hands and held them low to give Jay a step up to the basket. Jay sprang to the lip of the basket and pulled himself between the support lines and down inside. He grabbed the wooden box and stood it on end, shoving it to one side to clear as much room as possible for Fletcher Hall who was muscling his way up, elbows hooked over the edge of the basket. The man was short, but very strong, Jay noted. Hall grasped the lines and swung his legs into the basket that bobbed like a boat under their weight.

Just then an order was shouted by the lieutenant and the pistols of the defenders crashed as one. One of the horses stumbled and went down, pitching the rider over its head. The others saw the fire coming from the flatcar and swerved their mounts directly toward the express car.

"Cast off! Cast off!" Hall was yelling at the men below him. But everyone was looking the other way, crouching out of the line of fire of the attackers. Jay dug in his side pocket for his pocket knife. He got it out, snapped open the blade and leaned out and began sawing at one of the one-inch lines holding them.

"Stop it! What are you doing?" Hall screamed, grabbing his arm. "We'll need those lines later."

Jay snapped his knife closed just as Decker crawled over on his hands and knees and began to work on the knots.

The raiders were clustered at the express car, partially obscured from view. There was a lull in the firing because the defenders were short of ammunition and the attackers knew they were out of the angle of fire. Besides, Jay reasoned, the outlaws had the express car and that's what they had come for. Were they setting a charge to blow the safe? They must be convinced the defenders were only trying to protect their own lives and had abandoned the treasure. He glanced out into the desert and saw only the form of a dead horse to show for the three volleys from the protected defenders. It took an excellent marksman or a lucky shot with a handgun to hit anything as small as a man moving fast on horseback at forty or fifty yards. For whatever good it would do, Jay had given his shotgun to Roger Decker who, admittedly, wasn't much of a shot.

Decker was now joined at the other mooring line by Lieutenant Ormand. Hall was beside himself and almost jumped out of the gondola to help. "Why the hell did you tie them in knots that pulled tight? You idiots!" he screamed. No one paid him any attention.

The raiders swung their horses away from the express car and Jay expected to hear the dynamite blow the safe in the next few seconds. The riders weren't riding away from the train to get out of range of the impending blast or the defenders' fire. Instead, they were riding around the far end of the express car and coming toward them on the south side. Then Jay remembered and his heart sank. He had forgotten to close the safe after he had emptied it. He had blundered by not delaying them at all. One glance and they knew the treasure was gone.

Lieutenant Ormand saw them coming. He pulled the last of the knots loose and flung the line off. "Everyone on the other side! Quick!" he shouted, leaping up into one of the wagons.

The other mooring line remained fast as Decker scrambled away to cover. The two men in the wicker basket were suspended like targets in a shooting gallery. Almost without thinking about it, Jay had his Lightning in his hand and was firing over the rim of the gondola at the approaching horsemen. Then, a sudden, crashing volley of fire erupted from the guns of the defenders. The horsemen veered away, firing as they went. They galloped just out of effective pistol range and circled wide around the back of the caboose. It was obvious to Jay that the gunmen were convinced the treasure box was in one of the wagons on this flatcar or in the gondola, since the defenders were all clustered here.

Jay crouched to punch the empty shells out of his Colt. Hall was still cursing under his breath and firing. "You're not shooting up my gear and getting away with it!" he gritted as his .45 erupted. Pungent powder smoke blew back into Jay's face. "See what you think of this!" His eyes were blazing as he fired again. There was no fear in this man, Jay thought, as he squatted out of sight to thumb in fresh cartridges. Rage, not fear, was in those eyes and all because the robbers had the audacity to shoot at *his* balloon.

Jay, himself, felt coolly detached, as if he were watching all this happen to other people. He realized his heart was hardly beating much faster than its normal rate. He recognized the symptoms; the same phenomenon had often occurred just at the beginning of football matches and wrestling bouts during his college days. This peculiar ability to almost control his adrenalin and call on it for bursts of strength and speed may have accounted for his success as an athlete in track, wrestling, and football.

But this was only a fleeting thought as Jay cautiously raised his head above the rim of the wicker basket—a basket that would hardly slow a lead slug. Suddenly the basket lurched and they were airborne, shooting up and away on the stiff wind. Jay looked over the side. A man was clinging to the manila mooring line, about eight feet below the basket.

"Let go! Drop off!" he yelled, vaguely aware that Hall was also shouting something at his elbow. But, even as the words left his mouth, he knew it was too late. They were already nearly a hundred feet up, and rising fast. If the man let go now, he would very likely be killed. Jay saw puffs of smoke, but could not hear the shots as the robbers fired in their direction. The balloon made a big target. The disabled train was beginning to look like a miniature as it receded below and to the north of them. In an instant the scene was fixed in his mind's eye as if on a camera plate—the short string of cars, the upturned faces staring at them, the isolated locomotive, the blasted remains of the trestle. He had the strangest sensation, since they were moving at the same speed as the wind, that he was standing still and the earth and the train were falling rapidly and silently away from him. It made him slightly dizzy and he took an involuntary step backward from the rim of the gondola, holstering his Colt for fear of dropping it over the side. His movement rocked the basket and he grabbed the suspension lines to get his balance. Jay clung to the lines and looked up at the huge sphere that was bearing them ever deeper into the blue sky, a sky now shot with only a few ragged clouds. Then, somehow fascinated and repelled at the same time, he moved again to grip the padded edge of the basket and look down. The man was still clinging to the mooring line directly below. Hall's constant yelling was echoing in his ears, but his numb brain did not comprehend what the aeronaut was saying.

Fletcher Hall was shaking him by the shoulder.

"Dammit! Pay attention to what I'm saying! We've got to get that man up here before he falls!" He jerked Jay to the edge, rocking the gondola like a boat. Jay forced himself to look over the side once more. The figure still clung to the rope, but he had slipped down four or five feet and was slowly twisting around. The slim figure in the dark pants and jacket looked familiar as it sailed along against the background of the dun-colored, brushy landscape far below.

Then the man turned an anguished face upward between straining arms, and Jay felt an almost physical shock as he recognized the thief, Marvin Cutter.

Chapter Nine

"Hang on! We'll pull you up!" Hall shouted down.

Cutter continued to stare up with an expression that plainly implored them to hurry.

The rope was secured at the rim of the basket, then ran downward through a brass ring at the outside bottom before trailing more than a hundred feet off into space.

Hall turned to Jay. "Here, grab hold as far down as you can reach and I'll get a grip just above your hands," he ordered. "When I give the word, heave back as hard and as far as you can and hold it until I can get another grip."

Both men leaned over the edge and took hold.

"Ready?"

Jay nodded.

"Now!"

They pulled as one, leaning backward, legs and backs straining. It was heavy, but the rope came in a few feet.

Hall let go, leaving Jay to hold what they had gained and sprang forward for another handhold. As soon as he had a firm grip, Jay joined him and they repeated the process.

"Heave!" Their backs bent and they brought the rope in a few more feet over the lip of the basket.

The third time they leaned across, Jay saw Cutter's hands only about six feet below the bottom of the basket.

"I can't hold on." The man's head was down, but the weak voice still came clearly to them in the windless air. Jay saw his hands begin to slide slowly downward.

"No! Hold on! We've almost got you!" Jay shouted desperately. The thin hands continued to slide inexorably, his strength ebbing and his weight pulling him toward the final plunge.

"Don't jerk the rope. Just an even, strong pull," Hall gasped, leaning far out and wrapping his fingers around the line once more.

"Okay, now! Easy; don't jerk it out of his hands."

Jay's breath was coming quicker with the tension and the effort.

"Once more, and I think I can grab him," Hall gasped.

"Hold on!" Jay yelled again. "Just a few more seconds!"

One more heave brought Marvin Cutter's hands almost to the brass ring at the bottom of the basket.

"Can you reach him?" Jay asked, holding the slack they had gained and eyeing Fletcher Hall's efforts to stretch his five-foot, six-inch frame far enough out to reach the dangling figure. Hall hooked himself at the bend of his waist to the rim and leaned down. But even with his feet several inches off the floor, his hand was still a good foot short of the hanging man. For one terrifying second, as the basket jiggled, Jay thought the aeronaut was going to be overbalanced and pitched out, headfirst, into space. Jay quickly secured the slack of the line to one corner of the gondola where a shroud was attached. Then he grabbed Hall by the back of his belt and held him. Finally, the shorter man slid back inside with a grunt. His face was red and perspiring. "Can't get him."

"Let me try."

"No. I'm more used to this than you are."

Jay couldn't argue with that. "Is there something in here we can lower to him to grab?"

"There is," Hall nodded. "But he'd never be able to do it. If he lets go of that rope, even with one hand, he's gone."

Jay had to agree as he looked over the side again and saw Cutter's bloodless knuckles beginning to slip again. The man's head was up and he was looking at the basket like a drowning man at a lifeboat. But there was despair in his eyes, as if he knew he would never reach it.

There was a moment of indecision as the two men pondered their next move.

"If that rope didn't run through that little ring, we could pull him all the way up," Jay mused. "Look, I'm taller than you are by several inches. Hold my legs and let me try."

Jay could see that Hall was opening his mouth to object, but then finally closed it, and nodded. Jay stripped off his jacket and slid carefully over the padded lip of the gondola. He felt Fletcher Hall step between his feet and lock an arm around each ankle. Trying not to look down any farther than the dangling figure, he almost crawled headfirst down the outside of the basket. It would be up to this stocky aeronaut to pull both of them up once he got a grip on Marvin Cutter. Thank God the pickpocket probably didn't weigh more than a hundred and forty pounds with a full load of pilfered gold watches.

Now he was almost completely outside the basket, and his shins were hurting where the rim of the basket was digging into them, as Hall leaned back to balance his weight.

"Cutter!" he yelled.

His head came up and Cutter looked into his eyes, no more than four feet away. Jay reached for the thin wrists sticking up from the sleeves of the ragged jacket. He was still several inches short. He wiggled closer, conscious that Hall was locked onto his ankles with a death grip, cutting off the circulation. If he could just stretch a little farther! The blood was rushing to his head, and he could feel the pressure behind his eyeballs. He took a deep breath and strained. His fingers touched but he couldn't grip. He called on all his athletic ability. It became a personal challenge. This man would not die if he could help it. He knew he could reach farther if he tried with only one arm instead of both. He squirmed another precious inch or so out of Hall's grip and then let himself go completely limp, trying not to think of where he was, trying to concentrate only on the task at hand. Then he twisted slightly to the left and stretched as far as he possibly could, reaching down with his right hand only. He touched a hand, then his fingers closed around a wrist. He had him! But did he have the strength to hold him with only one hand? He gasped, took another deep breath and held it. The muscles in his back and arm strained as he pulled the dead weight straight up toward him. One inch, two inches, three. His head was pounding and his vision blurring. Through slitted eyes he saw where Cutter's other hand still clung to the rope. He continued to pull until every nerve and muscle screamed for relief. Then, with one lightning move, Jay's left hand shot out and gripped Cutter's other wrist, locking it securely. It was a catch worthy of a circus aerialist.

"Pull!" he managed to gasp. "Pull up. I've got him."

Hall began a steady pull on his locked ankles, and Jay gritted his teeth at the pain of his shins being scraped slowly across the rim of the basket and his knees being bent backward. Finally, his knees were over the edge and back inside and Hall pulled the rest of his body inside to counterbalance the body of the man still outside. The battle was won. Once Jay got his feet back on the floor, Hall reached over the edge and the two of them quickly hauled Marvin Cutter up the rest of the way. The thin man collapsed to the bottom of the basket, his face as pale as death. He lay there, half-gasping and half-sobbing.

Hall stepped to one side, trying to get a better look, but Cutter's tangled hair obscured part of his face.

"Who the hell is *he*?" he asked. "One of the passengers on the train? I sure don't remember him."

Jay quickly sketched in the details of Marvin Cutter and the reasons for his presence on the train.

Fletcher Hall heard him out without comment and then said, "That doesn't account for why he jumped on that mooring line as we took off."

"You'll have to ask *him* that," Jay said, slipping his arms back into his jacket. "As I told you, I lost track of him in all that hullabaloo."

Cutter did not appear to be in any condition for questioning at the moment. He still lay in a heap on the floor as Hall turned his attention to the flight of the balloon.

For the first time since he had seen Marvin Cutter hanging below them, Jay got a chance to look around. What he saw was magnificent. The sun was low on the western horizon, resting just above a line of low hills. To the north, at a distance of what must have been a hundred miles or more, he could make out the jagged outline of some green mountains. Beneath him, stretching for many miles in all directions, was a great valley, straddling the Continental Divide and covered with grass, tanning with the first frosts of autumn and sprinkled thickly with gray-green sage and greasewood. Just below was the winding trace of a road, faintly scratching the landscape. He guessed it might be the old stage road. The land showed small waves, or ridges, that Jay assumed must be higher than they looked from this lofty altitude. The planet was sliding steadily northward from under them. It was cool up here, and the low clouds had nearly all blown away to the south, leaving some mares' tails of high cirrus clouds streaking east and west. It seemed very odd to him, as he took a deep lungful of the clean air, not to be experiencing some sort of wind. But only a faint puff of a crosswind fanned his cheek now and then as the balloon and its cargo was being carried southeast at the same speed as the fresh breeze.

Jay took another deep breath and a shout of pure exhilaration burst from his lips. Hall and Cutter both looked at him as if he were demented, but he didn't care. He was giddy with the sheer joy of flying high and free. Miles and miles of mountains and plains were spread below him. No king could have felt mightier. And, best of all, they had gotten cleanly away from the raiders.

Jay turned to ask how high they were, and the question died on his lips at the sight of what lay south and east of them. Rugged mountains seemed so close he could almost make out individual trees. Conifers blanketed their massive slopes.

Fletcher Hall was also staring at this range of mountains, and then looking intently upward at the balloon and down at the rolling foothills that were steadily creeping closer.

Jay watched him for a minute, and finally asked, "What mountains are those?" As soon as he said it, the question sounded irrelevant. What he should have said was, "Are we high enough to clear them?" But he held his tongue.

Hall finally turned around, and realized what had been asked.

"Uh, I don't know. I don't have a map for this part of the country. I only carry detailed maps of places I'm expecting to be flying." His tone was sarcastic. He bumped his foot against Marvin Cutter who was now sitting up and looking around. "Get this man out of the way. I have work to do."

Jay slid his hands under Cutter's arms and helped him to his feet. Even though the man was relatively slight of build, Jay felt a twinge in the muscles of his lower back as he lifted. The adrenalin was ebbing and he was beginning to feel the effects of his mighty effort to save this man's life.

"We'll talk later," Jay said, looking into the lean face that was beginning to regain its normal color. The thief nodded, raking the hair back from his eyes and leaning back against the side of the five-foot-square basket. The inside lip of the basket was draped with several rows of sandbags, secured with twine. In each of the four corners was strapped an upright metal canister of compressed hydrogen gas—apparently for emergency use, as Hall had indicated earlier. Besides the tanks, the wicker gondola held a pair of field glasses Hall was presently using, two long, coiled ropes, a two-quart canteen that hung by a strap on one of the canisters, and the Wells Fargo box.

Marvin Cutter had slumped to a seat on the upturned treasure box, leaning his elbows on his knees.

Jay turned again to see how far they had come. In the distance he could just make out a straight line cutting across the high valley and then a slightly heavier line atop it that must be the disabled train. They had already flown a good fifteen miles or more. He pulled the Elgin out of his watch pocket. A few minutes past six. He had no idea what time it was when they took off. But, by looking straight down several hundred feet to the ground, he tried to estimate their speed. The terrain seemed to be flowing past at a pretty steady clip. It was hard to judge from this height, but he guessed they must be traveling at least as fast as an express train.

Fletcher Hall was still studying the mountainous terrain ahead of them through the field glasses, and ignoring the two of them as if they were not there.

Jay looked at the silent Cutter. "You want to tell me what you're doing here?"

Marvin Cutter raised his head and looked at Jay. "I had to get away," he said simply. "If I had stayed there, I would've had a hard time explaining who I was and why I didn't have a ticket after the excitement died down and those robbers got whatever they came for. Then, I would have been put off the train that came to rescue us, or they would have done some more checking and I'd a' landed in jail. They might even have mistook me for one of those masked robbers who got left behind." He shrugged. "When all that shooting started, I tried to hide. Then that dynamite blew the door off the end of the car. I was behind the freight on the other end, or I mighta been killed. Hurt my ears something fierce as it was. I slipped out and hid underneath. Just crawled along the ties under the cars until I got to the caboose and stayed there until the balloon was about to go. I saw my chance to grab on at the last second, but the knot came loose and it shot up so quick, I almost missed it. Just able to grab hold of the line."

"And came closer to gettin' yourself killed than if you'd stayed behind," Jay added.

"But I'm here now. You're responsible for me. I'm your prisoner, remember? You were going to turn me in at Omaha, so I guess I'm no worse off here." He managed a slight smile.

Jay didn't reply. Whatever fate was in store, the three of them were in it together—at least until this balloon landed, wherever and whenever that might be.

The sun was sliding down over the low mountains on the western horizon, suffusing the sky with red and gold. The clouds were nearly gone now, and the day was ending beautifully. Jay took another deep breath and tried to ignore the thought of where they might be going. He concentrated, instead, on savoring the moment—the great, panoramic view of the southern Wyoming Territory, the cool air, the breathtaking sunset. So far, at least, it beat being locked into an express car with nothing to see and little to do. What an adventure! Wait until he got back to San Francisco and told Fred Casey about this! It would make even Casey's job as a policeman in Chinatown seem dull by comparison.

His reverie was interrupted by the stocky aeronaut who bumped him aside to get hold of one of the dozen or so sandbags suspended inside the basket's rim. He hefted the bag up, worked open the drawstring at the neck, and spilled about half the sand over the side.

"Get over there and help me dump part of the sand from those other bags," Hall ordered.

For once, Jay didn't resent the peremptory tone. He saw immediately what was happening. They had to lighten the basket if the balloon was to gain enough altitude to clear the upcoming mountains.

Marvin Cutter sat on the upturned Wells Fargo box and watched them without moving.

Several minutes later the task was complete. Jay looked again at Hall for some sign that their efforts were having some noticeable effect on the balloon. Hall was intently studying the green bulk of the mountain range looming up directly into their path. Their only choices were to clear it or crash into it. It didn't appear that the wind was going to cooperate and change direction in time for them to fly parallel to the flank.

"Most of the time these air currents are in layers," Hall mused aloud, studying the ragged remnants of clouds above them. "Sometimes only a few hundred feet thick. If we can gain some altitude, I think we'll not only clear those mountains, but also pick up an eastward flow."

Jay took the field glasses and trained them on the mountains ahead. They seemed to jump close and frightening in the twin lenses as he adjusted the focus. He could identify spruce and fir in the higher elevations that were slightly above where the level flight of their balloon would take them if they stayed on their present course. Ridges of naked rock cut through the almost-solid covering of evergreens. Splashes of gold now took on the identity of isolated groves of aspen, their leaves a bright yellow with the coming autumn. On the lower slopes, thick stands of lodgepole pine thrust thousands of tall tops toward the sky. Jay had a sinking feeling in the pit of his stomach. He knew what a sailor must feel when gazing on the rocks of a lee shore. He lowered the glasses and the mountain range seemed to retreat to a safe distance. He took a deep breath and turned the other way.

"Can you still see the train from here?" Cutter asked, standing up. "What a view!" he exclaimed, finally overcoming his shock and fear and seeming to take an interest in his surroundings.

Jay brought up the glasses once more and looked back in the direction from which they had come.

The train was still visible as a dark line across the valley, miles to the northwest. He wondered if the people on the train could still see the balloon. At their height and in this clear air, he suspected they probably could. The balloon was still in the sunlight while the valley floor was now all in shadow as the sun dropped almost below the horizon. He adjusted the focus slightly and swept the glasses slowly back toward himself. Suddenly he checked them and looked again, finely adjusting the focus. There was a small dust cloud. Maybe a herd of wild horses; they were fairly common in this part of the country. But, as he looked, he saw that the horses had riders. And they were coming in a straight line, not veering at all. He lowered the glasses and could still see the small cloud of dust with his naked eyes.

The train robbers were still after them.

Chapter Ten

Hall looked at him curiously and then glanced back in the direction of the train. "They'll damn sure catch us, too, if we go down in those mountains," he grunted. "All they'll have to do is walk in and take the box, 'cause we'll be in no shape to stop 'em," he added, almost to himself as he turned back to studying the balloon and trying to gauge their speed and direction.

"We don't seem to be gaining any height," Jay ventured after a minute or two.

"We're not. Dump the rest of that sand."

In less than two minutes, all the remaining sand had been jettisoned, and the bags hung limply from their cords.

Jay and Marvin Cutter both watched tensely as Hall again scrutinized the underside of the balloon, the ground below, and the sky.

"Didn't do a damn thing," he finally stated. "That should have let us rise up several hundred feet. But, as far as I can tell, we're at the same height or lower. I have a sneakin' hunch that several of those bullets punctured the envelope. We're leaking gas somewhere, and it must be up higher than I can see."

"How big is this balloon?" Jay wanted to know.

"Average size. About forty thousand cubic feet. Big enough to make a good show and be visible at high altitudes, and small enough to be manageable, especially when it's time to pack up and transport it."

Jay noted the pride in his voice as he spoke of his flying machine.

"Can you use anything besides hydrogen in it?" Jay asked, more to keep his mind off what was coming than for information.

Hall leaned on the suspension lines and said, "Yeah. I've used coal gas from some of the gasworks in the eastern cities. It's cheaper and if it's for some big public celebration, they'll donate the gas as often as not. Doesn't have the lifting power of hydrogen, though."

Cutter had resumed his seat on the Wells Fargo box.

"But I won't have to worry about any public celebrations with this balloon anymore if we hit that mountain," Hall added, sadly. He seemed more concerned with the welfare of his equipment than he did with his own safety.

"Any chance we could get the gas in these tanks into the balloon?" Jay asked.

Fletcher Hall shook his head. "No way to lift those heavy tanks up there. But, most importantly, all the connections were left behind."

"Anything we can do?" Jay finally asked.

"Well, our only hope is to lighten this load. And, even then, we may not make it, depending on how much gas we're losing." He looked around him. "How heavy is that box?"

"That box isn't going over the side," Jay stated, flatly.

"I'm not talking about what's in it. I mean the box itself. We could dump the stuff into one or two of those empty sandbags."

Jay considered the idea for only a few seconds before pushing Cutter off the upended Wells Fargo box and fishing the padlock key out of his pants pocket. Cutter's eyes glinted at the sight of the stacks of greenbacks and bank notes and the soft clinking of gold coins inside the doeskin bags that Jay quickly transferred to the two canvas sandbags, pulling the drawstrings tight. He left the bags hanging by their cords to the lip of the basket. He lifted the empty wooden box by its end handles and balanced it on the rim of the basket, and gave it a shove. "There she goes. A good fifteen pounds lighter." He leaned over to watch the box sail, end over end, down and away from them. As it grew smaller and smaller, Jay got a sense of how high they really were. The empty box disappeared into the trees below. They were over the wrinkled foothills of the mountains. The land was gradually rising, and the balloon was gradually dropping.

"What we really need is to drop the weight of one or two bodies," Hall said.

Jay looked at him, sharply. "You got your parachute stashed in here?"

"In there." He pointed at a sealed container built into the side of the basket, the folding top of which served as a small table to spread navigation maps on.

"You actually thinking of jumping out of this thing before we go down?" Jay asked incredulous.

"I've never jumped in free flight before. Always stationary."

"I can't land this thing," Jay protested, fear beginning to tighten his stomach.

But Hall shook his head. "No, we'll take her down together. I'm not leaving my balloon, crippled or not."

"Let's drop these gas canisters," Jay suggested.

"Never!" Hall snapped quickly.

Jay said no more, but even to his inexpert eyes, unless there was a drastic change in the wind or lift of the balloon, there was no doubt they were going right into the side of the mountain. Since he was expecting no miracles, he was already preparing mentally for the inevitable. Their lives were in the hands of God, and of Fletcher Hall, who would need all his skill as an experienced aeronaut to set them down on this rugged, forested mountainside in a spot that would keep them from being killed. But Jay's heart sank as he looked again, for there appeared to be no open spots or grassy meadows on this side of the formidable range of mountains.

Suddenly, Jay felt the basket lift under his feet. The slight pressure was steady. "We're rising!"

Hall nodded.

Jay couldn't imagine why he wasn't excited.

"I was expecting it," the aeronaut said. "The air current is flowing up and over the mountain just like water flowing over a rock in a stream."

"We'll make it over, then?" Jay asked, hopefully.

Hall shook his head. "Afraid not. We're already too low. Look." He pointed up at the balloon. Jay could see the balloon had changed shape; it wasn't as distended. The wind had pushed the deflating envelope into a more elliptical shape. The cord netting was much looser than before. The gas was escaping too fast through the bullet holes. The raiders probably didn't know it yet, but they had shot the eagle out of the sky.

A forested ridgetop was coming toward them. The bottom of the basket brushed through the pine tops with a whispering sound and suddenly the valley floor was several hundred feet below them again.

"Throw those mooring lines over the side," Hall ordered. "We should have dropped them earlier."

Jay and Marvin responded quickly, gathering up the piles of loose line in the bottom of the basket.

"Make sure it's not tangled," Hall yelled, keeping his hand on the cord that connected the release valve. His voice was unnecessarily loud in the windless air, even though he had his back to them, looking ahead at the mountain.

Jay was dropping the line over the side, a little at a time, making sure the loops and coils fell out smoothly, without snarls.

"Quick, man! Get a move on!" Hall snapped, looking back over his shoulder.

Jay felt a flash of anger. If the man was going to use this line, why hadn't he said something earlier about coiling it down neatly? But this was no time to argue. So, keeping his voice steady, he simply asked, "What is this for?"

"It'll help slow us down. If it should snag in the treetops, it'll give us a helluva jolt, but it may stop us or slow us enough so we can descend gently."

Jay finally got all the line out—all three hundred feet of it. He looked over the side and saw it, along with the line Cutter had let out, hanging straight down and sailing along, well clear of the treetops. So they were still more than three hundred feet up.

Jay shivered and not just from the cold. The sun was below the rim of the world and, though the sky was still bright, the foothills below were in deep shadow as the early autumn night closed in. The darker it got, the tougher it was going to be to see, as Hall tried to maneuver as best he could to some kind of crash landing. As the deeply seamed and forested flank of the mountain came up to meet them, it seemed to be rushing by at a greater speed. Jay almost wished they were going in now. It was getting darker by the minute. He at least wanted to be able to see what he was going to hit.

He glanced over at Marvin Cutter. There was fear etched on the stubbled, pinched countenance. Jay looked away, thinking that his own face probably reflected the stomach-tensing fear he was feeling himself.

The air was still rushing up the slope, but the balloon was sinking even faster. Fletcher Hall had his hand on the cord that was releasing gas from the escape valve. If they couldn't ride over the summit, he at least would try to pick the place where they would come down. A glance upward showed the balloon being squashed into an elongated shape by the wind.

"Get a grip on those lines and brace yourselves," Hall ordered over his shoulder, keeping his eyes glued to the onrushing mountainside. "We'll be going in hard. There's a break in the trees and I think I saw a little meadow just beyond, but I couldn't be sure. I'll try to set us in there, but it'll be tough. I don't have much control. If we start to go into the trees, get down and cover your faces."

Jay and Cutter silently backed to opposite sides of the small basket and hooked their arms around the suspension lines.

Jay glanced over and down. The mooring lines were now dragging through the wind-tossed pines that were rushing past no more than ninety feet below them. Jay held his breath. At the speed they were going, it would be a miracle if they lived through this crash. The wicker basket would be smashed to pieces against one of those hundred-foot ponderosa trunks, and what was left of their broken bodies would fall through the limbs to the rocky slope below. Jay's knees were weak.

Something jerked at the basket, like a fish tentatively testing the bait on a line. Then a sudden and violent jerk nearly tipped the basket over as one of the mooring lines snagged below them. All three of the men were literally hanging by their arms on the lines as the basket lay on its side, the wind still pulling the balloon.

Before Jay could even get his feet braced, the line pulled loose and the basket shot forward, righting itself under the collapsing balloon. The last thing he was aware of was the onrushing of dark green treetops as the basket shot into the pines on the steeply-angled hillside. He shut his eyes and hung on desperately as they hit and then felt the gondola strike, throwing him sideways. The suspension lines cut into his arms. The basket spun, swung free for a second and then struck again and he felt the basket dropping. There was a crashing and smashing and stinging as tree limbs lashed his face and body. Then something hit the side of his head and his arms and legs went limp.

Chapter Eleven

He could have been unconscious only a few seconds, it seemed to Jay when he opened his eyes, but his next thought was that he was mortally hurt since he could hardly breathe and there was a sharp pain in his abdomen. Then he realized that he was hanging, draped over one of the suspension lines that was cutting into his midsection and restricting his movement. It was almost too dark to see anything, but he groped with his hands for the edge of the basket about a foot to his left. It was wedged at a precarious angle into the top limbs of a giant ponderosa pine. His head hurt where it had slammed into something and he could feel warm blood trickling down his face from his right temple. He uttered a silent prayer of thanks that he was still alive and, from what he could feel, not seriously hurt.

Moving carefully, so as not to slip, he moved his left leg and left hand back to the basket, and then very gently pulled himself back toward it, holding the line with the other hand. As his weight settled on the edge, the basket gave a lurch and dropped down about a foot. Jay's heart jumped and he grabbed for something to hold onto. But the basket didn't fall any farther. It was wedged at a forty-five degree angle, cradled by three branches near the top of a huge tree. The suspension lines were tangled in the conifer's limbs, and the lines and the balloon itself streamed off into the darkness somewhere beyond his sight.

Being careful not to shift his weight, he checked himself for any further injuries. Nothing appeared to be broken. His head ached. The scalp wound that had stunned him was bleeding freely, but otherwise he seemed to be sound.

Where was Fletcher Hall? And Marvin Cutter? Had they been pitched clear? Was he the only one left alive? For a moment he felt cold fear. The feeling was heightened by the sound of the chill night wind sighing through the evergreen branches with a noise like rushing water. He shivered. Then he felt his ankles turning on something piled in the bottom of the basket. He felt with his hands. Two of the metal tanks had broken their fastenings in the corners and were underfoot. Then his probing hands encountered a body under the cold metal of the tanks. He wished vainly for a light. His hands encountered the face and the stubbly beard and the long hair. It was Marvin Cutter. He let out a groan and moved slightly. He was alive. Jay pulled the heavy canisters off his legs and crouched to shove them back out of the way.

"Are you hurt?"

The answer was another groan and a deep sigh as Cutter pushed himself up to a sitting position.

"Are you all right?" Jay repeated.

"Yeah. I think so," came the whispered reply. "Kinda dizzy." He paused. "I was on the floor. One o' those tanks musta hit me in the back o' the neck. I can hardly move my head."

Jay reached down and took the small man under the arms and lifted him to his feet.

"Oh!"

"What's wrong?"

"Musta twisted my knee." He balanced gingerly on one foot in the canted basket and leaned on the edge with both arms.

"Where's Hall?"

"Down here," came the strong reply.

"Where?"

Nothing answered them but a grunt and a crack of a limb close by.

The basket rocked perilously as fingers gripped it.

"Give me a hand up."

Cutter hopped out of the way and Jay gripped the aeronaut's wrists and helped him work his way into the basket.

He brushed himself off and wiped a hand across his face. "Damn good thing that mooring line caught on something and snatched us up at the last second. Otherwise, we'd have hit a lot harder. Probably torn right through these limbs and hit a trunk—or the ground." He looked around, but the darkness now obscured everything. "Anybody hurt?"

"Nothing real serious. I got rapped on the head and Cutter had those tanks fall on him. Twisted a knee."

"Can you put your weight on it?" Hall asked.

A pause. "Yeah. Barely."

"Hope my balloon isn't torn up where it can't be fixed."

A stronger gust of wind swayed the top of the huge tree. Jay instinctively gripped the edge of the tilted basket. "Oohh! This is like being at the top of a ship's mast in a heavy sea."

"Be as still as you can," Hall said. "I don't know how securely this basket is wedged in here. We could still fall."

"We're a long way up," Jay said peering down into the rushing noise of wind-tossed darkness below.

"You can bet we are," Hall replied. "These pines get big. Could be a hundred, hundred-fifty feet or more to the ground."

"What now?" Jay asked. "We can't spend the night up here."

"Unless there's a storm brewing, the wind usually dies as the sun goes down," Hall observed.

But the wind, even though the sky was clear and speckled with stars, showed no sign of letting up. It was going to be very cold in this treetop tonight.

"See if you can pull in one or both of those mooring lines," Hall directed. "If they're not too tangled, we can use those to get down. They're plenty long enough."

One of the lines was hopelessly snarled in the trees behind them, and no amount of jerking and pulling could free it. It felt as if it were tied to a spring. It would come in a foot or so and then snap right back when the tension was released.

"Quit yanking on it," Hall said. "You might jar this basket loose. Here, I've got the other one."

He finished pulling it in, hand over hand, until the entire length of the three-hundred-foot rope lay piled around their feet. After some discussion, they decided not to risk letting the rope straight down from the basket for fear that their weight, jerking on the basket as each descended, might dislodge it and send it crashing down through the branches. Instead, Jay took the loose end of the line and crawled out onto a branch and made his way carefully in to the trunk of the big pine. The top of the tree was swaying in the stiff breeze and several times he had to stop and lock his legs around the limb and hang on as the top bent to a heavy gust. He closed his eyes in the windy darkness more than a hundred feet from the ground and felt an empty feeling in the pit of his stomach.

The gust passed and he scooted along the narrow branch to the trunk. He glanced up and could see the stars through the top branches. He guessed he was no more than a dozen feet from the top. At this height, the trunk was slim enough to wrap his arms around. He slid the loose end of the rope around the rough bark and began easing his way back to the basket, pulling the end of the rope with him.

Once back inside, Jay pulled the rope through to its end. They studied the problem of securing the line to something stable and finally decided to just drop it over the limb the basket was resting on and let it fall straight down. Even with a stiff neck and an injured knee, Marvin Cutter assured them that he could manage the climb down. Jay didn't doubt him. He had seen the little man hanging to the line in free flight and knew he was stronger than he looked with a wiry, whip-like strength. Jay couldn't wait to get on the ground and volunteered to go first. The wind was drying the sweat on his body and chilling him. His head was throbbing and his stomach was growling with hunger.

He slipped over the edge and made his way back to the trunk. Then he took a firm grip on the rope, pulled it tight, and began his descent, feet pressed against the rough trunk, and stepping on limbs where he could. He could see little or nothing, so he kept his eyes slitted against the pine needles and limbs that brushed his face. He paused to shake the line loose where it had hung up on a branch two or three times, but the farther down he got, the larger the branches and the thicker the trunk. He had never climbed down this distance before, but he managed to walk and slide and struggle his way down the trunk from limb to limb, the twigs scratching his hands and face. In a few minutes, his feet thudded on a soft, springy carpet of pine needles. He breathed a prayer of thanks. He had never really expected to arrive back on earth this gently.

"Okay! All clear!" he yelled up through cupped hands. He waited, unable to see or hear anything. He hoped the wind hadn't whisked his voice away. But shortly, the rope began to jerk and wiggle and before long,

Marvin Cutter slid down gingerly beside him and hopped out of the way for Fletcher Hall who arrived a few minutes later. Tied around his waist were the two sandbags filled with the contents of the Wells Fargo box. His field glasses hung down his back.

"Here, you can pack this," Hall said, untying the sandbags and handing them to Jay. Jay threw a quick loop in the cord to take up some of the slack and slung the bags over his shoulder. Jay was grateful that he and the others survived and also that the precious cargo entrusted to his care was retrieved and secure for now.

"Got any matches?" Hall asked.

Jay shook his head. Then, realizing no one could see the motion, replied, "No."

"I've got some," Hall said.

"Good. Let's see if we can find a break in these trees or some kind of a sheltered spot near some rocks and get a fire going," Jay said. He started down the slope, slipping and sliding on the slick pine needles. The other two followed his lead. Once his feet slipped out from under him and he sat down hard. He got up and paused to catch his breath as he waited for the other two.

"Where the hell you going in such a hurry, McGraw?" Hall grunted as he came up.

Jay didn't reply. He stood for a moment, trying to orient himself. He would continue downhill until the land either leveled off, or they broke out of these trees, or they came to a stream or some obstacle. He noted how still it was. He could hear the wind still sighing in the treetops far above them. He felt closed in and protected by the giant trunks. He loved the clean, fresh smell of pine. But his appreciation of this was tempered by the pounding in his head with every accelerated heartbeat.

"Hell, you've run off and left the skinny thief—uh, what's his name?"

"Marvin Cutter."

"Yeah. Did you forget he's got a bad knee? I was trying to help him, but you ran off in such a hurry, I had to catch up and tell you to wait."

Jay said nothing. He had just taken off down the slope and it was so steep, he had found himself going faster and faster, dodging among the widely spaced tree trunks. There was no undergrowth. It had long since been shaded out by this pine forest. But the way was often blocked with deadfalls—giant trunks lying on the ground or at an angle, caught in the live growth when they fell.

"We need to make sure which direction we're going," Hall said. "I want to be able to find my balloon again."

"If you're that worried about it, why don't you stay with it?" Jay asked, irritably, as they stooped under a massive trunk, Jay snagging his coat on the sharp point of a dead limb.

Hall just looked at him in the darkness.

"Unless you've got a compass, how are you going to tell what direction we're going? Can't see the stars and the moon's not up."

"I happen to have a compass in my pocket," Hall said, "but I'm not going to waste a match to look at it just now."

There was a scuffling in the dark as Cutter half-slid, half-hopped down the steep incline toward them.

He came to a stop and leaned against a huge tree trunk. He was breathing heavily, but he said nothing and made no complaint about being left. A man who had risked his life to escape with them wasn't going to start whining now. He was apparently used to taking whatever Fate dealt and making the best of it. He was the intruder here and, evidently, was not going to force himself in as an equal. The man was pitiful and suddenly Jay felt ashamed of himself.

"Come here. Put your arm around my shoulder," Jay instructed him, at the same time slipping his own arm around the other man's slim waist. "Let's go."

They started again.

Suddenly Jay felt a widening of the darkness around them. He stopped as Hall came up behind them. They had come out from under the trees and the slope had begun to level out under their feet. There was still no moon, but the starry night made vision barely possible. They made their way more carefully now and stopped only when Jay heard the gurgling sound of a stream ahead of them.

He unslung the canvas sandbags from his shoulder relieved to drop the burden. Although not particularly heavy, the bags had been causing the rope connecting them to dig into his shoulder. Then he remembered he had dumped two extra boxes of cartridges into the treasure box.

He made Cutter sit down on the ground while he went forward to the edge of the rushing mountain stream. Feeling carefully around the bank, he pulled out several good-sized rocks, brought them a few yards back from the stream, and formed a small fire ring. Then he walked along the edge of the stream, kicking here and there, until he found a pile of dead brush caught in a small evergreen by some past floodwater. He dragged out several armfuls and called to Hall to help him carry it back to the fire ring. With the dry tinder and handfuls of dead pine needles, it was no problem getting a fire started with the wooden matches Hall carried. There was still a fitful breeze, but nothing like the gale that had been blowing earlier. Maybe the weather was going to give them a little respite.

There was little or no talk as the fire was kindled. As it began to blaze and crackle, flaming up to push the darkness back a few yards around them, Jay could feel his spirits picking up as well. Cold, hungry, and tired as he was, as they all had to be, at least he was young and strong and had sustained no injuries, except the blow to the side of his head. Except for the dried blood matting his hair and the remains of a headache, he was none the worse for his experience.

"Wish we had something to carry water in," Jay remarked. He helped Cutter down to the edge of the stream where the three of them had a long drink and Jay washed the clotted blood from his head and splashed some of the ice-cold water in his face. Then they came back to sit by the fire, saying little, as they stared into the flames. Each man was intent on his own thoughts. But one among them had little worry about where they would go or what they would do next. Jay looked across the fire at Marvin Cutter, stretched out on his back, his jacket hugged about him, eyes closed and mouth agape. He was asleep. When you lead the life he has led, you learn to sleep anywhere and anytime the opportunity presents itself, Jay thought.

He, himself, was very weary. The stress and the fear were draining away, replaced by the warmth of the relaxing fire. He might as well sleep, too. There was nothing much they could do about finding their way out of here until daylight. He looked around for a soft spot to lie down on the grassy slope.

A branch cracked somewhere in the near darkness and he sat upright, reaching for his pistol. He and Hall scrambled away from the fire as the unmistakable sound of heavy footsteps crunched toward them.

Chapter Twelve

"Sounds like a bear!" Hall whispered as the two of them crouched in the darkness, guns drawn.

"Couldn't be attracted by the smell of our food," Jay whispered back, wryly. "And we're downwind of whatever's coming."

"Might be drawn by the light of the fire," Hall answered. "This is grizzly country. And I doubt if there's anything in these mountains that challenges them."

They paused, listening, but the noise had ceased. Whatever small sounds might be out there were masked by the rushing sound of the nearby mountain stream.

"We shoulda dragged Cutter outa there," Jay whispered.

"Too late now. Whatever's out there is just on the other side of the light now."

The footsteps had started again, and they could hear one every few seconds as a foot noisily encountered some loose rocks or dry brush. Whatever it was was making no attempt at silence.

Then the footsteps stopped again, very close, but just beyond the firelight. Jay held his breath, his Colt Lightning cocked. Silence.

"Hello, the fire!"

Jay jumped at the strong sound of a voice so near.

"Anybody here?"

"Move into the light!" Jay yelled, flattening himself on the ground in case the man fired at the sound of his voice.

Marvin Cutter had sprung awake at the first shout, and was crouching by the fire like a frightened animal, ready to flee. But Jay knew he couldn't move fast, the way he was favoring his injured leg.

There was a slight hesitation. Then a man stepped forward into the firelight, his hands held out from his sides, one of them holding a Winchester.

"Put the rifle down—slowly."

The man obeyed. Without being told, Marvin Cutter scrabbled over and pulled the weapon to him.

Jay and Fletcher Hall both got to their feet and approached, their guns trained on the intruder.

"Who are you?" Jay asked, eyeing the shabbily-dressed figure who stood about five feet, eight, but broad-shouldered and muscular. The firelight shone up under the slouch hat to reveal a face covered mostly with a full beard, trimmed short. He had a strong beak of a nose, topped by straight, heavy black brows.

"I was just coming up here to find out who you were," he replied, the deep voice resonating from his chest. He glanced at the two grim-faced men holding pistols and the figure on the ground, his own rifle trained upward, and apparently decided to expand on his answer. "My name's Vincent Gorraiz. Are you the men from the balloon?" He looked from one to the other.

"What if we are?" Hall answered. "You live around here? Where's your horse?"

"Got a mule, but he's back down in camp. Figured I could make this trek on foot in the dark better than he could. Saw your balloon go down in the trees. Thought I'd come and see if I could help. Anybody hurt?" He glanced at Cutter who still sat on the ground. He spoke in short sentences, like a man who didn't trust his voice to convey his train of thought.

"Yeah, we're the ones from the balloon," Jay said, easing down the hammer on his Colt and sliding it back into its holster. "Name's Jay McGraw," he said, thrusting out his hand. This is Fletcher Hall and that's Marvin Cutter. You a rancher around here?"

The bearded one answered with a rumbling laugh as he gripped each of their hands in turn. "Nope. Just the opposite, in fact. Just a sheepherder trying to stay out of everybody's way."

"You're lucky you weren't shot," Jay said. "That's not a good way to approach a strange campfire."

Gorraiz shrugged. "Thought about that when I got close. Thought maybe that fella on the ground was the only one here. Didn't hardly figure it to be cowboys chasing strays this far up."

"How do you know we're not cattlemen?" Hall asked.

"You don't have that look about you. Besides, we're pretty close to where that balloon went down. Figured it had to be somebody from that, if you weren't killed or hurt bad."

Jay noted that the man spoke very clear and precise English, but with a slight trace of a dialect he could not identify.

"Except for a twisted knee and a few scratches and bruises, we're okay," Hall said. "I've survived worse crashes than that. I'm a professional aeronaut," Hall answered with a trace of pride in his voice.

"Aeronaut?"

"A professional balloonist," Jay explained.

"What are you doing way out here?"

"We'll tell you all about it later," Hall said, impatiently. "Have you got any hot coffee at your camp?"

"Sure do. I forget my manners. I came up here to see if I could help. Put out the fire. I'll lead you down."

Cutter had not returned the Winchester. A good move, Jay thought. They didn't know anything about this man. This whole story about being a sheepherder might be a ruse. He might be waiting for a chance to kill and rob them. He could be some wild mountain bandit. Jay thought of the sandbags that contained the gold and bank notes. He was glad there were no identifying marks on the outside of the bags. He would make sure the bags stayed in his hands.

"We'll keep your rifle until we get to your camp just to make sure you're giving us a straight story," Jay said. Then he had second thoughts about leaving the rifle in the hands of Cutter. But he judged Cutter to be a sneak thief, not a violent criminal. Yet he might be desperate enough to use it to escape. If that happened, Marvin Cutter, the city-bred thief, would be on his own in the mountains with a bad knee. He had to believe the man would wait for a more propitious moment. But he couldn't be wholly certain, so he held out his hand. "I'll take that."

Cutter hesitated for a moment before he handed over the rifle. Jay cradled the rifle on the crook of his arm and slung the tied bags over his shoulder while Hall and Cutter kicked the rocks apart and scraped dirt on the fire.

"Lead on," Jay said, when the fire had been smothered to his satisfaction.

The moon was just beginning to appear above the trees. Once they got their night vision, the moon cast just enough light to be able to follow the broad back of Gorraiz moving down the slope in front of them.

Vincent Gorraiz led, followed by Hall helping Cutter. Jay brought up the rear with the rifle. His nerves were on edge. He worked the lever of the Winchester twice and ejected a cartridge into his hand, then slid it back into the loading gate. He was taking no chances; he intended to be ready for anything. He eased the hammer back down. It wouldn't do to trip in the dark and shoot himself or one of his companions accidentally. He swept his eyes back and forth and around for any sign of an ambush, but knew anyone lying in wait could be on them before he could react. The darkness was just too thick to penetrate.

Apparently, Gorraiz was very familiar with this mountain. He led them slowly, but unerringly, down the slope, sometimes descending a steep, rocky pitch where Hall, with the thief hanging on him, had to follow a step at a time. Fletcher Hall was grunting and puffing after a few hundred yards. Then the unseen trail leveled off and wound on a long, circuitous route through the trees, breaking out into an open meadow, and then back into the stands of big ponderosa that totally shut out any light, and they slipped and slid on the cushion of slick pine needles as the way led downward again. If there was any trail here, Jay could not detect it. Either this man had an uncanny sense of direction, or he was so familiar with this area that he needed no light, like a man finding his way through his own dark house at night.

They must have traveled a good two or three miles before they finally came out of the trees onto a gentle slope. By this time, Jay was helping the hobbling Marvin Cutter, and Fletcher Hall was following with the rifle. Gorraiz stopped and Jay paused. Cutter stood up straight with a groan, leaning lightly on Jay's shoulder.

Jay smelled the sheep before he saw them. Then he heard some faint bleating. He strained his eyes. There, in the middle distance, he detected a slight movement where the light from the rising moon was reflecting dimly from the gray-white wool of several hundred sheep.

"Chuck!" Gorraiz followed the low command with a quick, sharp whistle. An unusual whistle.

A few seconds later a dog came trotting up to him out of the darkness.

"This way." Vincent Gorraiz started forward again, the dog ranging at his side. He finally stopped about forty yards from the flock at a point where his gear lay scattered about near a fire ring. A slight breeze stirred the ashes and the red eye of a glowing coal was revealed. Gorraiz took a few sticks from the stack nearby and knelt by the fire, blowing it back to life. The new wood caught and flared up. Jay squinted at the blinding glare.

"Coffee will be ready in a few minutes," he said, amiably, setting a full pot on the small, iron, spider-shaped grid he set across the flat rocks. The pot began to steam quickly, giving off the delicious aroma of coffee. Jay suspected the man had just been preparing his supper when he saw the balloon go over and down and had quickly set the coffee pot on the ground, grabbed his rifle and started up the mountain toward the spot where he thought they had come down. Jay eased himself gratefully to the grass. He was feeling a lot more comfortable. Apparently, this man was just what he had told them he was—a solitary shepherd who intended only to help them.

"I've got some mutton stew if you're hungry," Gorraiz offered. Jay hoped he couldn't hear his stomach growling as he replied that he might have a bite or two if there was enough.

"I'm hungry as a horse," Hall replied, gruffly. Cutter said nothing.

Gorraiz set the small iron pot on the fire and went about cutting up a few more onions and potatoes into the pot. The stew was soon simmering and the aroma it gave off made Jay think he hadn't eaten in days.

"I've only got two cups and two plates," the shepherd said. "You'll have to share." He handed them the two tin plates and cups, and three spoons. He, himself, took the lid off the coffeepot and ladled in a helping of stew. After he had served his visitors, he used the spoon from the pot to eat with.

Jay thought he had never tasted anything as good as this stew. He could have eaten three times as much as the portion he got. But there was no more. Gorraiz had divided it equally and scraped out the pot. Jay was finished and sipping his coffee before the fry bread was finished cooking in the pan. Gorraiz forked out a smoking piece to him and he gingerly tore off a piece and dunked it in the black coffee.

"Who do you work for?" Jay asked, sitting cross-legged with his cup on the grass in front of him.

"My uncle."

"Who's that?"

"Milo Gorraiz," Vincent replied. "My father's younger brother."

"A family business, then."

Gorraiz nodded.

"Gorraiz is a funny name," Fletcher Hall said, in his bluntest manner. "How do you spell it?"

Vincent spelled the surname for him.

"Spanish?" Hall asked.

"No. Basque."

Jay had heard periodic tales of the Basque people. They had originated, as far as anybody knew, in the Pyrenees Mountains between Spain and France, and their language was unlike any other known. That accounted for the faint dialect. Jay had a sudden desire to know more.

"Were you born in the Wyoming Territory?"

The bearded shepherd shook his head. "California. My family came here about ten years ago when I was a young man. More have come since. Now I feel as if this is home."

"How long have your people been in this country?" Hall asked.

"Most of them came here from South America two or three generations ago. But we had been sheepherders for many years before that. It is in our blood. It has been our way of life for generations."

"Where did your people come from?" Jay asked, expanding on his earlier thought.

"As I told you—California."

"No, I mean, where did the Basque people originate?"

Vincent Gorraiz did not answer for several seconds as he pondered the question. Finally, he said, "No one knows for sure. We do not have a written history. The old ones who have handed down the tales of our past are not in agreement. Our language is different, our customs are different. We have lived in the Pyrenees Mountains for about two thousand years. Before that . . . ?" He shrugged. "It is a mystery, and one that is not likely to be solved."

Jay had heard that the Basques were very clannish, stayed to themselves, and preserved their own customs and traditions.

"Have you always been a sheepherder?" Jay asked.

Gorraiz nodded, staring into the fire. "Yes. Since I was a young boy. I feel that I have been at it all my life."

"Must get mighty lonely and boring, traipsing around the countryside after a bunch of smelly sheep," Hall remarked with his usual tact.

Gorraiz glanced up at him, and then back at the fire. "Actually, I prefer a little solitude to mixing with many of the people I have come across," he answered, pointedly. "Certain times of the year, such as at lambing time and shearing, it's hard work, no doubt about it. But other times, it's like caring for a bunch of children who are totally dependent on me."

An apt simile, Jay thought, considering how their bleating sounded so much like human cries.

"This life gives a man plenty of time to think and reflect on things," Vincent continued, removing his hat and placing it on the grass beside him. "I do a lot of reading—whatever books I can find and wherever I can find them. I am surrounded by this beautiful country, fresh, fragrant air, beautiful clouds and sunsets. Would not most men who live in the noise and dirt of the cities wish to trade places with me? There are trout in these mountain streams, my bedroom ceiling is spangled with stars, my clothing requirements are minimal . . ."

"Speaking of clothes," Hall interrupted, "how the hell do you stand it in the winter around here, living in the open like this?"

"One gets accustomed to camping out. I pick sheltered places, and I have warm fires and sheepskin-lined clothing. Even this beard is protection for my face for the coming cold weather. I carry what I need on my mules."

Jay had noticed the two mules picketed and grazing nearby.

The man spoke as if he were educated, even though he stated he had spent most of his life as a shepherd. Probably self-educated from the books he had read, Jay thought.

"Yes, it is a good life. I could ask for no better."

"Don't you ever miss seeing any women?" Hall asked.

Gorraiz nodded. "I will marry someday before long. It is my job to foster the flock and build it up so that when my uncle turns my share over to me, I will have earned it, and it will be enough to live and support a wife on. For now . . . it is enough. God has been good to me."

"Where are you taking these sheep now?" Jay asked.

"Autumn is coming on quickly. Chuck and I are bringing them down from summer pasture in the mountain meadows to lower ground for the winter. We will winter along the base of these foothills and in the small, grassy valleys that are protected from the worst drifts and winds."

Jay felt secretly glad that he was not facing the prospect of spending the winter outdoors on the Continental Divide. Whether he knew it or not, this man was a lot tougher than most.

The dog, Chuck, a black and white border collie, had not come up to share the light and warmth of the fire with the humans. Apparently, from good training, he lay quietly in the darkness about twenty feet away, head between his paws, facing the bedded sheep.

"Is this where you're going to spend the winter?" Jay asked, noting from the light of the moon that they were in some sort of long, narrow valley.

Gorraiz shook his head. "No. Farther down."

Vincent suddenly stopped and cocked his head to one side, his eyes probing the darkness. He looked toward his dog, who had raised his head, but still lay in the same spot.

Gorraiz got up and picked up his rifle.

"What's wrong?"

He stepped out of the firelight without answering, walked away a few steps and stopped, listening and turning his head this way and that. Finally, he came back and set the rifle down. "Thought I heard something. Must have been a prowling wolf or coyote," he said. But he still seemed nervous as he hunkered down by the fire and reached for the coffeepot. Jay noticed his glance flickering out into the darkness.

"Didn't rouse your dog," Jay observed.

"Oh, he heard something, all right," Vincent said. "But he knows better than to go chasing off after every sound or smell that comes along."

Jay saw the dog get up and trot away in a wide circle around the sheep. Gorraiz did not seem disposed to talk; he seemed preoccupied. A few minutes later the dog came back into view. He walked around in a circle a time or two and then lay down once more.

"I don't know where you boys are headed," Gorraiz finally said, to break a long silence. "But I'm going to have to be honest with you and tell you there may be more out there than just four-legged predators."

"Oh?"

"Yeh. There are some ranchers in this area who aren't sold on the idea of sharing the range with sheep. In fact, there are some that are downright hostile. If some of their hired guns come calling tonight, can I count on you boys for help?"

He looked at Jay, then at Hall and Cutter with large brown eyes under the thick brows. He was chewing his bottom lip. There was no fear—only concern and a quiet plea for help.

Jay felt his stomach tighten. What had they gotten themselves into now? Had they escaped deadly danger in the skies only to find themselves in even deadlier danger back on earth?

Chapter Thirteen

"This is not some practical joke?" Hall asked.

"I only wish that were the case," Gorraiz replied. "I started not to say anything about it, what with you being strangers here and all, and my guests besides. But I think it's only fair to warn there's at least a possibility of attack. Maybe it won't come tonight or next week, or next month, but it will come eventually."

"How do you know?" Jay asked, thinking that maybe this was just a touch of paranoia in a man who had spent too much time alone.

Gorraiz looked offended at the dubious tone of the question. "The Cattlemen's Association is big and powerful hereabouts. All of the big ranchers belong to it. They've got an interest in holding on to this free grazing land, and they're going to do it by any means, legal or otherwise. Lately, they've taken to bringing in hired guns to protect what they consider to be their land."

Jay had heard some rumblings of this growing dispute, gleaned mostly from back page articles in the San Francisco newspapers. But it was like reading of something that was happening in a foreign country and he had paid little attention to it.

"What possible harm could a few hundred sheep cause in a land this big?" Jay asked.

"It's not just a few hundred anymore," Gorraiz replied. "There are thousands here already and the number is growing every year as more herders realize there is plenty of good grazing here and good profits to be made. But overcrowding isn't the problem. The ranchers think the sheep eat the grass down too close to the ground so it ruins the range. There's even a notion that the sheep leave some kind of stink on the ground they've passed over so that no cattle will graze on it afterwards."

"Any of it true?"

"No. But when people want you out, they'll believe anything. The Cattlemen's Association is even calling the Basques a bunch of dirty, smelly foreigners. There are other men running sheep in Wyoming, too, but I guess the Basques are just easier to single out as a group." He shook his head, sadly. "Some of the herders have been attacked by night riders in masks. These men clubbed and shot a bunch of helpless animals and beat up the herdsmen. Warned them to leave the Territory or expect more of the same or worse."

"There's no way to compromise—maybe have sheep on certain areas of the range and cattle on another?"

"No. The ranchers were here first, so they feel the entire open range is theirs to use as they see fit, or to keep it clear of sheep until they decide to use it."

Gorraiz was silent for a moment, staring into the last flickering flames of the dying fire. The light reflected on the bold profile—the strong nose, balanced by the thick, black beard.

"I am a simple man with simple needs," he went on. "I want to take care of my own business, and let others do the same. Yet . . . this whole idea of tending cattle—surely a humble occupation such as my own . . . I can't understand why the cowmen act as if they are lords of the land and rulers of all they can see and touch." He spread his arms wide as he spoke. "Is it because they sit high atop a horse and look down on other men afoot? Are we lesser men for that? Are we servants or peasants to do their bidding?" His voice rose with indignation. "I am a peace-loving man, but I swear I will kill the first man who tries to harm my sheep or me."

"No sense getting yourself all worked up," Fletcher Hall said, gruffly. "Nobody's bothered you yet, and I doubt anything will happen tonight."

Jay nodded in agreement. This man had been alone so long he apparently welcomed any friendly face so he could talk and unburden himself of his hopes and fears. Except for a question or two or a remark from the three of them, Gorraiz had done all the talking.

"If it will ease your mind, we'll stand guard tonight," Jay offered. Even though he was far from full, the warm stew and two cups of black, hot coffee had revived him. "I'll take the first watch."

He got to his feet and rinsed his cup in a small bucket of water nearby, then set the cup on a stone of the fire ring. As he did so he caught Hall's eye. The aeronaut was plainly disapproving, as if he saw no need of a night watch, and was irritated that Jay had volunteered him for it. His red, puffy eyes were almost crying out for a good night's sleep.

The food and coffee had given Jay a boost of energy so he felt he would be alert for at least two hours. Besides, he didn't want the agony of being awakened once he got to sleep. Then again, there might not be much sleep in this camp tonight, anyway, if Gorraiz had no spare blankets. It would be the grass for a mattress and the sky for a cover, and plenty of cold air in between.

Hall had taken the bucket of dirty dishes to a stream that bisected the little valley to wash and scour them with sand, grumbling all the while that not only had Marvin Cutter come along uninvited, but now was worse than useless with a bad leg.

At the edge of the light Gorraiz was feeding the dog with some sort of dried food from the big pack.

"I'll wake you in two or three hours," Jay said as Hall returned to the fire.

Hall nodded. "There's a single tree about forty yards out that way where you'd be out of the moonlight."

"Good. It'll be a couple of hours before the moon goes down behind the hills."

Jay hefted the rifle and glanced at the dying campfire. He motioned for Hall to step away from the light with him.

"Forget about Marvin Cutter standing watch. I don't think he can be trusted. I don't think he'll try to get away, since he can't run. I just don't want him to be tempted to rob us or take those two sacks and slip off into the dark."

"Hell, I wish he would escape. He's been a damn nuisance so far," Hall snorted.

"Well, we're stuck with him now. He'll look for a better opportunity. He's not real fond of the wild. Personally, I don't really care what happens to him myself, but I'm sworn to protect what's in those two sandbags. That's the reason we went to all this trouble . . ."

"And wrecked my balloon and almost got us killed," Hall finished.

Jay ground his teeth to keep from making a retort. Instead, he said, "I'll take the sacks with me on guard. If anything should happen tonight, they'll be in the low fork of that tree." He pointed at the lone tree where it made a blot of shadow on the moon-silvered field.

Hall grunted his assent and returned to the fire circle where Gorraiz and Cutter were settling in to get some sleep. The Basque rolled into a sheepskin-lined sleeping robe. The herder had supplied Cutter with a spare blanket, Jay noted as he moved off. He took up a position by the solitary tree, a young oak that had somehow taken root here. He flung the bags over the lowest limb and settled down to watch. After the camp had quieted for the night, Jay could hear the soft gurgling of the small stream nearby. The wind had finally died, and the three-quarter moon was shedding its reflection on the valley, bathing everything in enough light to see indistinctly. Jay stayed in the black shadow cast by the tree and carefully scanned the valley. The sheepherder had chosen his campsite well. Here was plenty of grass and water. The sheep were all fairly bunched and lying down. The dog was resting somewhere beyond Jay's vision. Even the hobbled mules finally stopped grazing. One stood quietly and one lay down. The scene was as peaceful as anyone could want. Jay leaned his back against the rough bark and scanned the valley carefully. If there was any trail or road through here, he was unable to detect it at night. Vincent Gorraiz obviously knew his way around, even in the dark. If any attack came, it wouldn't necessarily come by road, but that was most likely. Any night riders would not be afraid of being heard as they rode up. They would be strong in numbers, and wouldn't bother trying to ride cross-country through the woods. Most likely it would be swift, relying on the element of surprise.

Jay could feel himself relaxing. After about an hour, the effects of the coffee began to wear off, and his eyelids grew heavy. He tried walking around the tree, stretching his tired muscles, yawning, pressing the cold metal of the rifle against his face. Finally, he slid to a sitting position, his back against the tree, the rifle resting across his raised knees, and tried his best to focus on staying alert.

It seemed he had only blinked, but when his eyes flew open, he knew he had been asleep. The moon was down behind the hill and a coyote was raising a long, mournful howl in the distance. Jay shivered at the dampness and struggled stiffly to his feet. He had been lucky. He had fallen asleep on watch, an inexcusable blunder that was punishable by death in the war-time military. He took a deep breath of the chill air to clear his head. No one had attacked. He had gotten away with it. He didn't know what time it was, but it had to be time to awaken Hall to take the next watch. The nap had refreshed him and the cold made him more alert. He walked slowly around the tree, gripping the clammy rifle, senses alert for any unusual sights or sounds, while his mind worked on other things.

Where would they go from here? Maybe they could get directions from Gorraiz to the nearest town or ranch and strike off walking. He would surely know where the nearest ranch was. Maybe they could buy some horses and ride out. But they had no food or water for any long trek on foot. And Cutter was not up to walking any distance. This might be a good chance to leave the thief behind with the shepherd. That way Cutter could escape by his own devices whenever he got ready, and Jay McGraw and Fletcher Hall would not be held responsible—if anyone ever heard about it. Surely someone would be looking for them. The men on the train had seen them fly away, and knew generally which direction they had taken. Then a disturbing thought came to him. It was a memory that had been lurking in the back of his mind since before the balloon had crashed. That memory was the view through the field glasses of several mounted men riding hard in the same direction their balloon was flying. He had not been able to make out their faces, but it had been the same number of men—seven—who had attacked the train the last time. Of course, he told him-self, the riders might have been some cowboys who saw the balloon in the sky and were riding to catch up with it, just out of curiosity, since such a sight was unheard of in this part of the country. But he could not convince himself. If the men were the would-be robbers, why were they so persistent? True, there was probably $30,000 plus in bank notes and gold in the two sandbags. A goodly sum, to be sure, and one that any gang of train robbers would risk much for. But, to have at least two or three of the gang wounded and then see the contents of the Wells Fargo treasure box suddenly fly away in a balloon, of all things, would surely be enough to discourage most men. But maybe they knew the Eagle could not fly far since they had shot it full of holes and were like hunters pursuing the quarry until it falls from a mortal wound. Whatever the case, Jay knew, deep within, that those riders had been chasing the balloon and might, even now, be camped within a few short miles of them, awaiting daylight to start the search anew. The thought crossed his mind that maybe he was getting paranoid, just like the sheepherder was about an imminent attack generated by the Cattlemen's Association. Maybe the responsibility of all this money made him more nervous than he should have been. Maybe his imagination was just overactive. But then, it had not been his imagination that had stopped the train and blasted the express car. He shook his head. No need to be worried about things he couldn't figure out. His main concern now had to be getting this treasure back in safe hands and the three of them back to civilization.

It was time to prod Hall up to take the watch for the rest of the night.

Chapter Fourteen

"Try some. It's very tasty."

The cheery voice of the sheepherder penetrated Jay's consciousness and he forced his gritty eyelids open a crack and rolled over, hugging the blanket around him. He had used Hall's blanket when the latter went on guard duty sometime earlier. He didn't know how long he had slept, but it wasn't enough. In spite of the hard ground, Jay felt as if he could use another hour or two. But the smell of something cooking and the cold air brought him awake. He threw off the blanket and reached for his shoes.

It was daylight, but the sun was still well down behind the mountains to their backs. A low ground fog lay in wispy patches along the valley floor. Most of the sheep were on their feet and quietly grazing on the dewy grass. Gorraiz was squatting on his heels by the fire, stirring something in a small pot. Hall was kneeling on one knee, watching the proceeding. He looked tired and out of sorts. Marvin Cutter, silent as usual, sat cross-legged on the ground, a blanket draped over his narrow shoulders.

The bearded shepherd looked as if he had not bathed or changed clothes for some time. But his hands and nails were surprisingly clean, Jay noted as Gorraiz dipped out a glutinous mixture from the pot, flopped some on a tin plate, and handed it to him.

"What is it?" Jay asked, taking a spoon and preparing to sample the hot food.

"Dried fruit. I just mixed it with water to boil it and soften it up."

"What's it called?"

Gorraiz shrugged. "Don't reckon it has a name. Just a mixture of wild plums and grapes and some berries."

"Not bad," Jay remarked, tasting the slightly tart mixture.

"It's better with a little brown sugar, but I'm out of that," Gorraiz answered.

"How do you make it?" Jay asked, noting the unappetizing purplish-gray color. Hall was dabbing at his small portion with a sour look on his face.

"I cook the fruit to the consistency of a thin paste, then put it through a sieve to strain out the seeds and stems and stuff, then spread it out on a flat platter by the fire to dry it. Looks like pieces of leather when I get through. It won't spoil and it's light and easy to carry. Wards off scurvy through the winter, too."

Hall had set his plate on the grass and was sipping dourly at a cup of coffee.

"What the hell's wrong with this coffee?" the short aeronaut growled, spitting a mouthful to one side.

"We drank the last o' the regular coffee last night," Gorraiz answered. "Should have warned you. I've been up in the mountains all summer and I've run short of provisions. Had to make this coffee up myself."

"Another one of your original recipes, I presume?" the redheaded aeronaut growled.

Jay had to turn away to hide a grin. This man was used to putting on his aeronautic demonstrations before large crowds, being treated as a celebrity, and wined and dined at receptions and dinners by civic leaders wherever he went. Substitute coffee was not something he was eager to become accustomed to.

Gorraiz ignored the sarcasm and said, "Not original with me. Just mix two tablespoons of molasses in about a gallon of bran, parch it good until it's brown. Then use it like you would roasted and ground coffee beans. Some favor roasted dandelion roots, but I like this better, when I can't get the real thing."

Hall made a face, but gulped the bran coffee without further comment, then reached in his coat pocket for his pipe.

Cutter ate his meager fare and even asked for a little more, which Gorraiz supplied proudly.

Hall stood to one side, puffing on his pipe as Jay and Vincent washed and stowed the camp gear. The blankets and sheep robe were rolled and stuffed into one of the bulky packs. As the pack lay open on the ground, Jay saw at least four books inside that were adding to the weight the pack mule had to carry. Food for the mind, Jay thought. As he slipped his blanket inside, he surreptitiously glanced at a couple of the titles. *Don Quixote* was the largest volume. Another was *Diseases and Treatment of Domestic Sheep.* Jay couldn't see the others before Gorraiz came over and stuffed in the frying pan, clean coffeepot, tin plates and cups that rattled together in a cotton flour sack.

The fire was doused with the dishwater, and the black and white border collie, Chuck, had the flock moving down the valley before the sun had topped the mountain. Gorraiz had offered to let Marvin Cutter ride the saddle mule, since he still claimed to be unable to put weight on the injured knee. The thief accepted as if it were his right, without a word of thanks. The rest of them walked, following the sheep, who moved along at a leisurely pace, grazing as they went. The rifle was slung in a sheath on the saddle mule. Jay carried the sandbags with the bank notes and gold and the extra .38 caliber ammunition slung over one shoulder. It was uncomfortable, but he was determined not to let the bags out of his possession.

Jay and Fletcher Hall both wore their Colts. It was a beautiful fall morning, and Jay had to force himself to think in terms of danger. Summer was making a last fling along the backbone of the continent as the sun came up to warm the valley. The mountains appeared completely deserted. The foothill valley they were descending was devoid of any human traces. It was as peaceful a pastoral scene as he could imagine.

But Jay also saw the fresh hoofprints of many cattle. The grass and water were good here in this valley and probably in others like it in these foothills. They would offer considerable protection from winter blizzards. If Gorraiz intended to winter in this area, Jay could see why there would be trouble.

"How about telling me again how you got here?" Gorraiz asked abruptly as they walked along.

Jay went over the story, adding more details of the attempted train robbery and their escape in the balloon.

The sheepherder was incredulous. He pushed his hat back on his head and glanced sideways at Jay. "Mr. McGraw, I may be a simple sheepherder, and live my life mostly away from people, but that's a tall tale if I ever heard one. Why don't you tell me where you really came from?"

Jay had lost his cap that identified him as a Wells Fargo messenger. He took a chance and pulled one of the canvas sacks open and took out a bound stack of bank notes.

The sheepherder's eyes widened at the sight. "If that's real, that's more money than I've ever seen in my whole life." He looked dubiously at Jay, then averted his eyes, saying nothing more.

Suddenly Jay understood. "You think we're robbers, don't you?"

Gorraiz did not reply.

"Wish there was some way I could prove our story."

"That's no Wells Fargo sack," Gorraiz said, indicating the canvas sandbag.

Jay explained that they had jettisoned the green and white Wells Fargo treasure box. He went on to explain who Marvin Cutter was and how he happened to be with them. Vincent Gorraiz nodded. "I reckon that story is so fantastic it has to be true." He glanced at the slim back of Martin Cutter who was astride the slow-walking mule a few rods to one side of them. Jay followed his glance and wondered if the herder was looking at Cutter or at the rifle that hung in its sheath beneath the rider's right leg. Leaving the rifle on the mule with Cutter was probably not a good idea.

Then Jay remembered he still had his Wells Fargo badge pinned to his cowhide billfold. He pulled the billfold out of his hip pocket and showed the silver badge to Gorraiz. "All right. I believe you." He jerked his head at Hall who walked a few steps behind them. "He's not with Wells Fargo, then?"

"No. He just happened to be on the train and was hauling his balloon back east. He's a professional aeronaut. Ever seen one before?"

"No. That balloon was the first I've ever seen."

"He performs for big crowds. People pay to come and see him. He even jumps out in a parachute from a thousand feet or more."

"What's a parachute?"

"Sort of a big canopy made of silk. He hangs underneath from ropes. It floats him down to the ground like a leaf from a tree."

Jay almost laughed at the look of disbelief on the Basque herder's face. He had to be careful not to push this man's credulity too far, just when he had gotten him to believe their story. Now that he had him convinced, the next job would be to convince him of the urgency of their situation. They had to get to a town that had a Western Union office to telegraph his company of the safety of the contents of the express box.

"Where's the nearest town from here?"

"Rawlings." He pointed in a vague northwest direction. "Probably forty miles or so as the buzzard flies—or the balloon," he added with a wry smile. "Maybe fifty or more the way you'd have to go."

"Any ranchhouses closer?" Jay asked, indicating the hoofmarks of the cattle.

Gorraiz shook his head. "Those prints don't mean anything. Cattle wander all over this range for hundreds of miles around. But there does happen to be a ranchhouse maybe eight, ten miles from here. But you don't want to go there. That's the Jacob Wright place. If they even suspect you've been around me, they're liable to shoot you on sight."

"Just point us in the right direction," Hall said, joining the conversation. "They won't know where we came from."

Vincent Gorraiz shook his head again. "Old man Wright has a nose like a coyote, I hear. He'll *smell* sheep on you."

"Doesn't matter," Hall said. "We need to get back. Maybe this Wright will have some horses we can borrow or buy."

"I wouldn't bet on that," Gorraiz said. "Old man Wright has a fearsome reputation. He doesn't like any strangers on what he considers his land. I don't think you'd get a very warm reception."

"We could appropriate some horses at gunpoint, if he won't sell," Hall said, his face turning red in the early morning rays of the sun.

"I wouldn't try that. He's got some mean gunhands working for him."

Jay was eyeing the mule that Cutter rode. Maybe Gorraiz could be persuaded to part with it for a price. They could make it to Rawlings, taking turns riding the mule and walking. Maybe the mule could carry double if he wasn't pushed. A thought flashed into his mind. He remembered seeing Cutter sitting cross-legged on the ground this morning. Hardly a position a man would take who has an injured knee. He wondered how badly hurt this sneak thief really was. He tucked this bit of information in the back of his mind for future reference.

"What mountains are these?" he asked Gorraiz.

"The Sierra Madres. There's a bigger range on east about forty miles. There are some well-watered valleys in between the two where Wright runs a lot of cattle. They don't bother me much if I stay up on summer range in the mountain meadows. But more sheep are moving onto the range in the southern part of the Territory, and I hear from my uncles that the Cattlemen's Association is pushing to clear the range of all sheep. Now that I'm coming back down to winter range, I expect trouble. Bad times coming." He shook his head sadly.

"Can't your uncles help you?" Jay asked.

"They've got flocks and families of their own to look after farther north—two or three days' ride from here. I've got a cousin at Medicine Bow who helps me now and then. But I doubt if I could depend on him in a fight, even if he was here. In fact, he's supposed to meet me down this way in a week or so and bring me a few supplies. I can't leave these animals to go into town. I trust Chuck to take care of them, and have left him alone with them for a couple of days at a time, but it's just too dangerous now. I think you boys should stay with me for a few days. When my cousin comes, he'll have a wagon, and you can ride back to Medicine Bow with him." His tone indicated this was the simplest and most obvious solution.

Jay considered this for a couple of minutes. The time and place of the expected meeting with this cousin seemed very vague. He chafed at the thought of the delay. But, on the other hand, it sure beat walking all the way to Rawlings. It was possible that Gorraiz just wanted them to travel with him for protection against attacks by the cattlemen's gunhands he seemed certain were coming. This thought rankled. Jay had seen quite enough gunplay for a while. The three of them had been extremely lucky that they had not been shot during the holdup attempts. He wanted no more confrontations if he could help it.

"We'll give it some thought," Jay replied, noncommittally. For some reason he could not fathom, he felt uneasy. Maybe it was the weight of responsibility for the Wells Fargo bank notes and gold. Maybe it was the presence of Marvin Cutter. Maybe it was the proximity of the Jacob Wright ranchhouse and gunhands Gorraiz had told them were determined to run him off the range. Whatever the cause, Jay had a sinking feeling in the pit of his stomach. He would not mention it to Hall for now. The aeronaut would probably blame the feeling on the dried fruit concoction they had eaten for breakfast. But the feeling persisted as the morning wore on, and Jay caught himself unconsciously loosening his Colt in its holster.

Chapter Fifteen

It was the dog who gave them the warning. Before any horsemen were heard or seen, Chuck began moving the flock toward the sloping hill on the southeast side of the valley. When his woolly charges didn't move fast enough, he darted from one to another of the stragglers, nipping at their hind legs.

"Somebody's coming," Gorraiz said. "The three of you better hide in those trees until I see who it is."

"There's no road through here, so it's no traveler just passing through," Vincent said at Jay's questioning look. "And we're on land that Jacob Wright claims as his own."

Before he had even finished speaking, Jay and Fletcher Hall were jogging after the sheep with Marvin Cutter following quickly on the mule. When they reached the treeline, Cutter slipped off and hobbled into the growth of young pines that hid the three of them from view.

Just as they crouched out of sight, Jay heard the muffled drumming of hooves on the grassy earth. In less than a half-minute, several horsemen trotted into view around some low hills from the direction the flock had been headed.

They reined back abruptly to a walk at the sight of the bleating flock of two or three hundred sheep. Some startled sheep bolted away, but Chuck quickly rounded them up and brought them back with the rest. The dog nervously paced back and forth, watching the approaching horses, head erect and alert.

Gorraiz had stopped, calmly awaiting the approach of the four riders. He made no move toward the rifle that still rested in its saddle scabbard on the mule. As the men reined up and the lead rider dismounted and walked toward the sheepherder, Jay caught his breath. It was the same man who had dynamited the small bridge at the train. He recognized the bow-legged stride, and the leather vest with the silver conchos the man wore. If these were the attackers, where were the other three? There had been seven men during the last attack.

"Howdy," Bowlegs said, stopped a few feet away.

Gorraiz nodded in greeting, but said nothing.

"We're looking for two, maybe three men who are probably in this general area. You seen anybody since yesterday?"

"No. Nobody. Just my sheep and my dog."

Jay's stomach was in knots.

"I know it sounds funny," Bowlegs went on, with a humorless half-grin, "but these men probably came down in a balloon on the side of the mountain back here."

"A balloon?" The sheepherder shook his head solemnly.

"Where were you camped last night?" one of the men still on horseback asked.

"Back up this valley a ways," Vincent said, pointing over his shoulder.

"And you didn't see a big gas balloon flying over just before dark?" the mounted one persisted, dubiously.

"If there was such a balloon, I must have been asleep already, or was busy cooking my supper. I wish I had known about it. I've never seen a flying machine such as that before. Where did it go?"

"That's what we'd like to know," Bowlegs said, gruffly. "I hope you're not lying to us, sheepman. If we find out you are, we'll be back here, and there may be nothing left but your dog to take care of these sheep." Bowlegs swung into the saddle and the four of them trotted off, up the valley and deeper into the foothills.

Gorraiz signalled for them to stay hidden for two or three minutes after the sound of the hoofbeats had completely faded.

Jay felt shaken when he got to his feet and came out. But he tried to hide his feelings by remarking lightly to Hall, "They're sure going to a helluva lot of trouble to get at what's in these sacks."

Hall looked at him and then up the valley where the men had disappeared. "Are holdup men usually that persistent?"

It was the very same question Jay had been asking himself since he had seen the horsemen through the field glasses from the balloon.

"I don't know."

"They're not after you, personally, are they?" Hall asked.

Jay shrugged. "I don't think so. They have no reason to be. Even without their masks, I didn't recognize any of them. I wonder where the other three went. There were seven of them."

"Maybe split up to comb these foothills."

"Maybe we're overlooking something . . . or someone," Hall said, turning toward the silent Marvin Cutter. "You said this man was hidden in the express car, and that's what they attacked. We all assumed they were after the contents of the safe. Maybe they were after the notorious thief, Marvin Cutter, for some reason. What about it?"

Cutter shook his head. "I never saw those men before. Sure, I have my share of enemies, but most of them are on the side of the law. If they're after me, I don't know why. Could be 'most anything," he grinned, his gums showing pink through the growth of black stubble.

"I doubt they were after him," Jay said, thoughtfully. "Remember, the lieutenant just managed to throw that stick of dynamite out the door that had been planted next to the safe."

Hall was unconvinced. "Could be the gold in that safe was just an added bonus—you know—as long as it was there."

"Look, gents, if you think it's me they're after, I'd be glad to ride on outa here and not inflict myself on you anymore. That is, if you want to pay for this man's mule. If not . . ." he shrugged. "With my bum leg and all, I may have to stay with you for a time."

Jay wondered just how "bum" that leg really was. If Cutter was exaggerating his injury, why? What was his motive? This whole thing was very confusing. He couldn't fit the pieces together. Was there any relationship between this thief from the city who had stowed away and the train robbers? Was Cutter just an opportunist who was planning to stay around, pretending to be an invalid, so he could seize a chance to make off with the sacks Jay carried over his shoulder?

Gorraiz whistled a signal to Chuck and the collie started the flock leisurely down the valley again. Cutter remounted the mule with help from

Jay. Gorraiz took his rifle from the scabbard and carried it cradled in his left arm. He would not be caught unawares again. "Sheep-killing gunmen come only in the dark, with masks," he remarked. "But now I will be ready for anything."

The Winchester was an 1873 model. It was not a carbine and was relatively heavy, but the stocky Basque carried it as if it weighed nothing.

When the sun was high, they paused to rest in the shade, but not to eat. They sprawled on the grassy slope under the trees and sipped water from the canteens, before refilling them from the clear stream that still meandered along their course as the valley flattened out.

Jay set the sacks on the ground beside him. He could not get his mind off the robbers who were still chasing after the contents of these sacks. If the estimated $30,000 was split seven ways, that would only amount to something over $4,000 each. A goodly sum, but was it really worth all the trouble they were going through to get it? Was it just the money, or was it something else? Jay had pondered it, and pretty well convinced himself that Cutter had nothing to do with these robbers. But, if not the thief, and possibly not the money, what then? The robbers must have somehow gotten misinformation about the amount of treasure the train had been carrying. They must have thought it was much more.

Idly, he pulled apart the drawstrings of the bags and dumped their contents out onto the grass. There were the stacks of crisp bills, the leather pouch of gold coins, some official-looking, gilt-edged stock certificates in a small folder inside a large brown envelope, a small, sealed tube, wrapped and addressed to a James Simpson at the Excelsior Hotel in Chicago. Any return address? He turned the light tube around. Only "J.O. Brown" with "San Francisco" scrawled underneath it. Did he dare open it? No; that would violate everything the Wells Fargo Company stood for— safe, speedy delivery of any merchandise entrusted to the company. That certainly meant no tampering with packages by company messengers or anyone else. But these were extraordinary circumstances, he reasoned, turning the sealed tube over in his hands. Surely it would justify just looking inside to see if this might be the one thing the robbers were after. But if he were wrong, it could very well cost him his job when the company found out.

To hell with it, he decided. If what he had been through in defense of company cargo and property wasn't proof enough of his loyalty, then Wells Fargo could have their job and be done with it. He ripped the paper wrapping carefully off the end of the tube and shook it. Nothing came out of the hollow, bamboo shoot, so he inserted his finger and pulled forth a folded slip of paper. He could feel Hall's eyes on him, but he didn't look up as he unfolded an oblong piece of pale blue stationery. On it was written in a bold, black script, "Palace Windsor Twelve Oaks."

The cryptic note made no sense to him. He handed the paper to Hall who read it silently and handed it back.

"What do you make of it?"

Jay shrugged. "I thought it might give some clue as to what these robbers were after. It's obviously some sort of shorthand that will mean something to this James Simpson it's addressed to. Means nothing to me."

"Whoever Brown is, I wonder why he didn't send his four-word note by telegraph. It would have been a lot quicker and cheaper. Looks like he started to address it for the U.S. Mail, but gave it to Wells Fargo instead."

Marvin Cutter was sitting in the grass on the other side of Jay with his injured leg stretched straight out. He reached across and picked up the bamboo tube and looked closely at the handwriting on the address and the name, "J.O. Brown." Jay, surprised at the thief's interest, reached to take it back from him, and saw Cutter's face go deathly pale. The container dropped to the grass between them, and Jay thought the man was going to faint.

"What's wrong? You all right?"

Cutter swallowed hard, nodding as he did so.

"What's wrong? Did you see something on there? What was it?"

Cutter shook his head and passed a hand over his eyes. "I'm all right. Got a little dizzy there. Must be the pain in my knee."

Jay got the note back into the tube, tucking the paper carefully around the end, hoping it might look as if it were just scuffed in transit. He returned the bank notes and gold to the two empty sandbags, as they got to their feet and prepared to move on.

Jay, watching the small man out of the corner of his eye, saw him take four normal steps before he suddenly began to limp heavily again.

As Jay boosted him back up onto the mule, he silently resolved to insist on taking a look at that knee as soon as they made camp for the night. He might not be able to tell much about it, but he could see if it were swollen. It was obvious to Jay that Cutter had recognized something about the writing on that address that had shaken him severely. So severely, in fact, that he had totally forgotten to limp on the leg that was supposed to be injured. He hoped he was not seeing ghosts where there were none, but one way or another, he was going to get the truth out of this Marvin Cutter before another day passed. Had he known what was ahead, he would have forced the truth out of Marvin Cutter at that moment.

Chapter Sixteen

Even though they were on edge and alert the rest of the afternoon, they saw no more of the train robbers. The riders had either taken another route down out of the mountains, or were still up above them somewhere, searching for the downed balloon.

"Where are you taking these sheep?" Jay asked as the sun was sinking low on the horizon.

"We'll camp just a little farther on. Tomorrow I want to go a few more miles. There's an old log cabin that was built by a mountain man about fifty years ago. Nobody lives there now. If the place is livable, I plan to shelter there during some of the worst winter weather. That's where my cousin and I plan to rendezvous when he finally gets here with the supplies."

"I thought you lived outside all winter," Jay grinned at him.

"Not if I can do better. My wool doesn't grow as thick as theirs. I hear a man over in Rawlings has built a little cabin on a wagon bed that he's trying to sell to one of my people up north of here. I haven't seen it, but the blacksmith who made it claims it's the greatest thing for sheepherders. Take your house with you. No more sleeping on the ground in the cold and cooking over a campfire. It may catch on, but the only problem I can see with it is it can't be driven into the mountains where I take my flock for summer grazing." He shrugged. "Besides, I'm used to being outside all year long."

The weathered skin of his hands and face above the beard were ample proof that he rarely spent any time under a roof.

"It will be nice to get in out of the deep drifts if we have some bad blizzards this year."

"What about the sheep?" Jay wanted to know. "They don't look like they could survive on their own." As soon as he said it, he knew he was showing his ignorance of sheep raising. But Gorraiz didn't seem to mind. In fact, the more the Basque talked, the more fluent he was becoming, and the more he enjoyed the conversation. It was as if his vocal mechanism was finally sliding together with oil on the machinery after months of rusty disuse. Jay noticed his halting, short sentences had grown into longer, more involved utterances.

"Oh, sure, the sheep can survive on their own, as long as my dog and I are nearby to keep them bunched and look after them. See, most of them are Churros, a breed brought by the Spaniards almost three hundred years ago. They're tough. They winter well. To get a little more meat and a different, thicker wool, I'm experimenting with crossbreeding. See that big fella over there? That's an expensive Merino ram my uncle bought to upgrade the stock. Maybe in another year or two, he'll produce enough good crossbred lambs so I can turn back a good profit to my uncle and get a flock of my own. I love this solitary life," he said, glancing around at the beautiful foothill valley, "but I don't plan to live this way the rest of my life. I don't want to be chasing these animals when I'm a lonely old man with the ague in my bones." He grinned, showing white, even teeth. Somehow, Jay could not picture him as a decrepit old shepherd as he watched the powerful, thick-muscled figure stride along, staff in hand. "It's hard work sometimes, with the lambing and shearing seasons, but there's plenty of time the rest of the year for just taking it easy and reading and thinking and enjoying the beauty of all this." He gestured at the green hills and the mountain range behind them.

"I want to thank you for what you did for us back there," Jay said after a few minutes. "That took a lot of courage to face up to those men."

"I didn't like the look of them," Gorraiz replied. "I just played dumb. I'm good at that. But I don't think they believed me. They'll likely be back, especially if they find your balloon. They know you'll have to be on foot around here somewhere, without food. You could have gone in any direction. They may be on the other side of the Sierra Madre by now, or searching these parallel valleys that drop down from there. But when they don't find you, they'll be back, sooner or later. There's plenty of water around here, but nothing to eat this time of year, unless you can survive on grass like my sheep. But we can fool 'em again. We just need to look sharp to make sure we see them before they see us. Any chance your people or friends will come looking for you?"

"Oh, there will be a posse or some Wells Fargo men out combing these hills when they find out what happened, and determine that we didn't get across this mountain range. It might take a few days before they catch up with us, though." Jay spoke with a confidence he didn't really feel. He still had that premonition of disaster gnawing at the pit of his stomach.

Less than an hour later they went into camp in a grassy area, near a thick stand of young pines on a nearby slope. They built a small cooking fire only a few yards from the trees and picketed the two mules close at hand. Gorraiz placed the flock between them and the stream, which still flowed along about fifty yards away. It ran silently, or gurgled over and around some large rocks, but it had lost the force of its current here on the flatter valley floor. The stream was bordered with willows and a few low trees, but their view was relatively unobscured to the southwest for a couple of miles where the valley lost its identity and merged with the drier, upland desert floor, studded with sage. Not much was said about the selection of the campsite, but it was obvious Gorraiz was aiming to provide them with the best and quickest cover available should it be needed.

As soon as the homemade aparejo was off the pack mule and the rider and saddle off the other, Jay approached Marvin Cutter who had limped over and eased himself to the ground in the soft grass out of the way.

"Lemme see that knee."

Cutter looked up, surprised at the abrupt command. Without a word, he began sliding up his trouser leg. Jay gingerly probed and squeezed the ligaments on either side of the joint. Cutter caught his breath in sudden pain two or three times.

"Stand up."

Cutter struggled to his feet.

"Stand up straight on it."

Cutter stood.

Jay slid up the other trouser leg and compared the size of the two knees.

As near as Jay could tell, they were as skinny and symmetrical as a pair of knees can be. He could not detect the slightest swelling. There was a purple bruise about the size of a half-dollar high on the calf of the right leg—the one Cutter claimed was injured.

"Okay." Jay walked off.

There might have been a very slight stretching of the ligament, Jay guessed, but he suspected it was more like the thief had sustained a bruised calf, saw a chance for some sympathy, and faked a more serious knee injury from the heavy metal hydrogen tanks falling on him. A desire for more sympathetic treatment, or simple laziness so he wouldn't have to share in the work, and could ride the mule—it had to be one or more of these motives. Well, the man had not survived in San Francisco for several years as a thief, burglar and pickpocket because he was forthright and honest. Jay often had to fight his tendency to treat everyone at face value. If a man was friendly and sociable on the surface, he found himself, more often than not, trusting him and distrusting someone like Fletcher Hall, who was arrogant and overbearing, but, in reality, was probably honest and totally reliable. But he had found, since coming west more than two years before, that there were all kinds of men here, and it was the general practice to take men at their word unless they proved themselves to be other than they seemed. But one had to be wary. By the time a scoundrel showed his true colors, a trusting individual could well be fleeced of his money, wounded, or dead. There were slick card sharps, and confidence men and criminals of all types, from cutpurses like Marvin Cutter, to the gangs who robbed banks, stages, and trains. It seemed, on this trip, that Jay was having to deal with outlaws at both extremes.

But his growling stomach told him it was time to put that kind of thinking aside for the time being and get on to something more immediate and practical—like supper.

Gorraiz had a pot of stew simmering over the fire in no time. This time its main ingredient, he told them, was venison jerky from a deer he had shot a few weeks earlier in the mountains. It was not his practice, he said, to eat any of his sheep unless no other food was available. These sheep were to sell, not to consume.

"Besides, I really get attached to them after a while," he said, leaning back against his saddle on the grass and spooning up a mouthful of stew. "They're almost like my own children."

Jay could see his point as he watched the docile creatures being herded here and there by a single dog on verbal and hand-signalled commands. The soulful eyes and the bleating in his ears all day had left him feeling as if he were in a children's nursery.

"I'll help you stand watch tonight," Gorraiz said, as they finished up, cleaned and put away the tin utensils. The coffeepot still steamed on a flat rock by the fire.

"Good enough," Hall said. The aeronaut's appearance had weathered to the hue of his surroundings. His celluloid collar was missing, and the front of his white shirt, showing through the tan corduroy coat, was dingy with dust and sweat. It all blended in with his rust-colored hair, ruddy complexion, and red beard stubble.

"Might be a good idea if you three slept back in the trees a ways, out of sight," Gorraiz said. "Just in case we have a surprise visit by that bunch that came through today."

The night promised to be clear and calm, Jay noted as he carried a blanket back into the evergreens. And the night air had not begun to chill as rapidly with the disappearance of the sun as it had the night before. They were a few hundred feet lower than previously. That, and the absence of wind and the protection of the stand of pines, would make for a somewhat warmer night, even this far above sea level at the beginning of October.

Gorraiz had opted for the first watch, Hall would take the midwatch, and Jay had the deadest, darkest hours just before dawn. Marvin Cutter again had all night in.

Later, Jay would question his own judgment in allowing the sheepherder to take the first watch. He might have guessed if anything was going to happen, it would happen in the hours before midnight. But he, himself, could not resist the chance of getting several hours of uninterrupted sleep. He reasoned that when he was awakened for the early morning watch, the chill would probably have already driven him out of his blanket.

But his well-thought-out plan was not to be.

He was in an unusually deep sleep when yells and the crashing of gunfire brought him straight up. He threw off the blanket and snatched at the gunbelt that lay by his head. By the time his hand closed on the butt of the Colt Lightning a few seconds later, the fog was gone from his brain and his alert eyes were probing the inky blackness. He could hear someone scrambling around a few feet from him. The frantic bleating of the sheep was punctuated by the snarling and barking of the dog. Jay crouched, gun in hand, trying to focus on what was happening. Everything was in turmoil. He could just make out mounted figures riding past what was left of a very low fire. He staggered blindly down the slight incline through the snatching limbs of the small evergreens toward the open campsite. He heard more yelling and cursing. Jay threw himself on his belly just at the edge of the trees as the shooting started again. Muzzle flashes showed they were firing into the panicked flock. Where the hell was Gorraiz? Or Hall, or whoever was on watch?

"Shepherd, this is your last warning!" a voice yelled. "Next time it'll be you instead of these stinkin' woolies! You understand?"

"Hell, he probably don't even understand plain English, Jim. He's one o' them greasy Basque bastards."

Jay could hear their voices moving around as their horses shied and danced around at the sound of gunfire. But there was no moon and the glowing coals of the dying fire gave almost no light, at least not enough light to shoot by.

"Where the hell is he?" a third voice asked.

"Damned if I know. But he's gotta be around here somewheres."

"Let's plug a few more of these sheep and get the hell outta here. He may be drawing a bead on us right now."

"More likely hidin' somewhere or hightailin' it as fast as his legs will carry him," came a guffaw.

"I still don't like it. Let's get going."

Jay cocked his Colt and strained his eyes in the direction of the voices. But they kept shifting and he couldn't make out a thing.

"Get off this range, shepherd!" the first voice yelled. "This is Wright land and you're poisoning it with these stinkin' sheep!"

A pistol roared twice. This was what Jay had been waiting for. He fired at a spot just above and to the left of the flash. An instant later another shot cracked from the trees to his left.

"Ah! Gil, I'm shot!"

"Hang on!"

"Let's ride!"

Hoofbeats drummed on the grassy earth and suddenly the horsemen were gone.

"Hall?"

"Yeah. I'm over here. Where's Gorraiz? And Cutter?"

"I don't know, but we got one of them."

"I heard him yell, but he must have stayed in the saddle."

"Be careful until we're sure they're gone," Jay cautioned as Hall went to the campfire and started throwing on some dead brush and wood that lay nearby. The fire blazed up as the brush caught. Hall stepped back away from the heat and light as Jay came up.

"They're gone all right. It took the fight out of them when we drilled that one."

"Gorraiz! Where are you?"

They ignored the bleating, milling sheep and the white lumps of wool that lay still here and there as they moved out in a widening circle, yelling for the sheepherder and Marvin Cutter.

"Hey, McGraw, I only see one of the mules. Weren't they both hobbled?"

"Yes. I don't think he could have broken loose. I put on those hobbles myself. And surely Gorraiz wouldn't have ridden off on him."

"Hell, they both seem to be gone," Hall said, walking back out of the trees after a quick inspection in the near-darkness.

The black-and-white border collie came trotting up, whining.

"Where are they, Chuck?" Jay said, uttering the question aloud. The dog pricked his ears forward and looked at them with intelligent eyes, as if he understood the words. He whined again.

"How many did they kill?"

"I don't know. Maybe a dozen or more," Hall replied, squinting past the glare of the fire at the prostrate piles of wool. From where he stood, Jay could see red stains on several of them.

"Oohhh!"

Jay's heart jumped at the sound and he spun around, reaching for his holstered Colt.

Chapter Seventeen

Jay jumped away from the firelight, aiming his Colt at the bearish figure lumbering toward them from the trees.

Then he let out his breath in a rush and holstered his gun as he saw Vincent Gorraiz staggering toward them, holding his head.

"Are you shot?" Hall asked as both of them rushed up to aid the sheepherder whose knees were beginning to buckle. They caught and eased him to the ground. By the wavering firelight, they could see that one side of his face was bloody. Jay's stomach was in knots.

"Where'd they get you?"

The brown eyes flickered open. "I wasn't shot. Someone hit me. What happened? Were we attacked?"

"Yes. Didn't you hear them or see them?"

"No." Gorraiz struggled to sit up.

"Just lie back and take it easy."

"I'm all right. Just dizzy. Oh, my head!"

"Get him a drink of water," Jay said.

Hall grabbed the bucket and jogged off toward the stream.

"You may have a concussion. You hurt anywhere else?"

Gorraiz attempted to shake his head, but grimaced at the pain of the motion.

"Just stay still and see if you can remember what happened," Jay said.

"I let the fire die down and I was on guard at the edge of the trees back there where I could see the flock and the valley. Couldn't see much of anything, though." He paused, and took a deep breath, as if talking were a great effort. "Don't remember much after that. Something hit me from behind. I went down and out. Next thing I know, I woke up just now. Feels like somebody cracked my skull."

"Your flock was attacked by at least three mounted men," Jay said. "They shot some of your sheep, and they were yelling at you the whole time. So I guess it couldn't have been one of them who hit you."

"Oh, no!" Gorraiz raised himself to one elbow and looked toward the flock. "Oohhh! They got my Merino ram."

"I couldn't see who they were," Jay said, apologetically.

"Doesn't matter. They probably had masks on. Cowards always wear masks," the Basque muttered with a groan.

Hall arrived with the bucket of water and, using the shepherd's own bandanna, began washing the blood off his face and cleaning the matted hair.

"Have you seen Marvin Cutter?" Jay asked.

"No," Gorraiz replied, his eyes closed.

Jay left them and walked away toward the trees where they had been sleeping. He rubbed a hand across his eyes and his stubbled cheeks. He had been tired before, and now was doubly so since the adrenalin was ebbing after the excitement of the attack. Everything seemed to be going against them. And yet he felt powerless to do anything about it. He really didn't understand what was happening, or why.

When his eyes had again adjusted to the dark, he found one mule, still hobbled and grazing peacefully. The other mule was nowhere to be found. Jay briefly considered fashioning a torch from the fire to inspect a little more carefully, but rejected the idea. The small pines were so thick, he would run too great a risk of starting a forest fire. He realized he didn't need a torch to tell him that Marvin Cutter was gone, and was riding the missing mule. He had been the one who had hit Vincent Gorraiz, even before the attack. It was the only logical explanation.

With a start, he remembered the sacks with the Wells Fargo treasure. He fumbled to the place he had been sleeping and found them where he had flung them when he jumped out of his blanket. He thrust his hands into each bag. As near as he could tell, nothing was missing. After a more thorough inspection, he discovered the rifle was gone, along with a blanket, most of the remaining venison jerky, and a canteen. Cutter had taken just enough to survive and had made his break. Except for the stolen mule and rifle, it was good riddance as far as Jay was concerned. He returned to the fire where Gorraiz was sitting on his sheepskin sleeping robe and holding his wet bandanna to his forehead. He was feeling nauseated, he told Jay in reply to his query. Jay relayed what he had found.

"Glad to be rid of the man," Hall remarked, echoing Jay's thoughts.

Gorraiz lay back on the robe, the wet cloth pressed to his forehead and eyes.

Hall drew Jay aside. "I got the bleeding stopped, but he has a nasty cut on the crown of his head. Big knot. Except for his hat and the thick hair, he might have been killed or hurt a lot worse."

"Wish I had my hands around the throat of that little weasel," Jay gritted through clenched teeth. "But I didn't figure him to be the violent type."

"Desperate to get away, I guess," Hall said. "He knew he was going to jail when we got him back to civilization."

"Well, where do we go from here?" Jay felt unutterably weary.

"First thing we need to do is keep him awake the rest of the night. If he's got a severe concussion, we don't want him to go to sleep. He might never wake up."

Jay nodded. That meant no sleep, but they needed to stay alert for any further trouble, anyway. He really did not think there would be any more nocturnal visitors, but his hunches had been wrong before.

They put the coffeepot on and prepared to take turns walking Gorraiz around and talking to him. During the long hours that followed, they drank innumerable cups of black coffee and poured several down the injured sheepherder as well. The stimulating effects were probably nil, since it was only the parched bran coffee they were drinking.

By the gray light of a cold mountain dawn, they broke a skim of ice on the water bucket, poured it over the fire, packed up the remaining mule, and helped Gorraiz aboard to ride bareback just forward of the pack.

Fortunately, Chuck was so well trained he needed no directions to start the sheep moving once more. Gorraiz indicated the direction they were to take to the abandoned mountain man's cabin. They left the carcasses of the dead sheep lying where they had fallen, food for the coyotes, wolves and buzzards. Jay was secretly glad that none of the poor animals had just been severely wounded so that none of them had to be put down with a bullet from his own gun. Men who would shoot dumb animals just to get at their owner were the lowest of the low. They would stop at nothing. Well, at least one of these hired guns paid the price by stopping one or two slugs. This whole business of fighting over the open range was ridiculous, Jay thought. But greed knew no bounds.

By mid-morning they had found the abandoned cabin. It was backed against a steep hillside and faced a gently sloping, short-grass meadow that ended at the creek, two hundred yards away. The long-gone mountain men had chosen well for a place to build. The back of the one-room log structure was protected from the northwest by the hillside. It was situated near grass and water and protected on three sides by large cottonwood trees. In fact, if Gorraiz had not directed them, Jay could very well have missed the cabin, so well was it hidden in the trees and brush that had grown up around it.

Gorraiz was still feeling the effects of his concussion, so Jay helped him off the mule and into the cabin. The remainder of the flock spread out and went to grazing peacefully on the grassy meadow as Chuck circled to keep them contained in the immediate area.

The door of the cabin was missing, but someone had hung a piece of canvas from the top of the doorframe to cover the opening. Inside, Gorraiz walked slowly to one of two bunks, saw that there was no mattress and said, "I think I would rather lie down on the grass outside in the shade."

Jay dutifully helped him back outside and found a shady spot to spread the herder's blanket, and Gorraiz eased himself down onto it with a soft groan. "I think I'll just rest a little while," he murmured with closed eyes.

Fletcher Hall walked up, leading the mule with the pack still on its back. "What's the plan?" he demanded in his usual abrupt manner.

"We can rest here. The sheep will be all right. Chuck will keep them close," Gorraiz muttered almost unintelligibly as he faded into sleep.

Jay and Fletcher Hall looked at one another and Jay motioned for him to move back toward the cabin, away from the sleeping man. They went through the hanging flap of canvas into the low room.

"He needs rest," Jay said. "And this is probably the best place around here for him to get it. He seems to have all his wits about him, so I guess there was no serious damage. It'll probably take a few days for that head to heal up. He's pretty tough. He'll be as good as new."

Hall shifted his weight from one foot to the other and leaned heavily against the post of the bunk beds. "And just what do we do in the meantime? Stay here with him? Go for help? Maybe fortify this cabin against another attack? What if those men who attacked the train come this way again?"

"You're asking all the questions," Jay retorted. "Why don't you try supplying some answers? Do you expect me to make all the decisions?"

"This is your play. You didn't hesitate to make the decisions back at the train—decisions that got my balloon wrecked and got us in this mess."

Oddly enough, this reply did not even irritate Jay. He hardly heard it; he was thinking about what they should do.

The injured man could not be left alone for at least a day or so until he could take care of himself. Even then, Gorraiz would be in danger from any night riders who wanted to gun down his sheep, or him. One man would be helpless against several mounted gunmen. If the Basque's cousin was expected to meet him here in a few days and bring some supplies, perhaps the two of them could defend themselves and the sheep, or move out of the area. He silently ground his teeth in frustration as he pulled over a homemade wooden chair and sat down.

Gorraiz had not been in any hurry to get out of the area of the Jacob Wright ranch. It was as if he had a fatalistic attitude about it. He certainly couldn't be thinking of challenging the power of the big rancher who apparently claimed these foothills and grazing lands for miles around. Whatever range Wright ran his cattle on was appropriated by prior right of occupation, and woe to the man who said otherwise. As long as Gorraiz was in the mountains on summer range, there was no contact and no problems, since the cattlemen had no reason to covet the high mountain valleys and meadows. But now that the sheepherder was coming down to winter pasture, the trouble had started.

Jay shook his head and looked up. Hall was sitting glumly on the edge of the lower bunk, smoking his pipe and staring at nothing. Jay's eyes fell on the two sandbags he had draped over his knee when he sat down. He had been so busy worrying about Gorraiz and his sheep and the raiding cattlemen, he had almost forgotten about the Wells Fargo treasure that he somehow had to protect and get back safely. He wondered if the train robbers had given up the search for them yet. It was very likely they had found the downed balloon tangled in the big pine trees, but only an expert tracker could have followed their trail over the carpet of soft pine needles and the rocks and brushy meadows where they had gone from there. One thing was sure—he and Hall had to stay near cover as they worked their way back toward the railroad or Rawlings. If they were caught out on foot in the open, it was all over. Maybe they could travel at night over the plateau and sleep under the thick sage during the day until they reached a town on the railroad. But that was a very chancy thing. What were the alternatives? Staying here until they were found by a posse, or someone a little less friendly? Wait for the herder's cousin to show up with a wagon as Gorraiz had suggested? That might be another week or more, if at all.

He took a closer look at the interior of the cabin. Someone had made this place fit to live in, and it had been done in the recent past. Some of the rotten shelving had been replaced with new wood. The chair he was sitting in had been repaired with a brace made from a fresh sapling. Canned food was on the shelves—tomatoes, beans, and pickled beef. And the tin containers were only barely speckled with rust. They had not been there long. The canvas that hung in the door frame was even fairly new. Unless Gorraiz or some other herder had done this, it had to have been done by some of the hands from one of the ranches in the area, very likely someone from the Wright ranch, since they were probably no more than a dozen miles from the ranchhouse, as Gorraiz had described it. If the ranchhands used this place for shelter or sleeping, Gorraiz appeared to be bearding the lion in his den by stopping here also. It was almost as if he wanted to provoke a confrontation. Even though the stocky Basque was a quiet man who enjoyed reading and meditating on the beauties of nature, Jay had the feeling that he was not one to let someone push him around, if he felt he was in the right. This whole question of who had the right to the public lands would have to be settled sooner or later, and it was clashes between men like Gorraiz and Wright that would probably force the issue and eventually decide it.

Jay got up and walked over to the crude rock fireplace at the end of the room. No attempt had been made to repair its crumbling mortar, but fluffy ashes remained in it. No rain down the chimney had yet compacted them. Some remains of burnt cigarette papers littered the puncheon floor. He turned away with the uneasy feeling that he wanted to get out of here.

"I think we should leave tonight," he said to Hall.

"And go where?"

"North. Toward the railroad. We'll take one of the canteens. It may take us two or three nights, but we'll hit the railroad and then follow it east toward Rawlings."

To Jay's surprise, Hall got up, sucking at his pipe that had gone cold and said, "I'm ready. I can't wait to be gone from here." He knocked the dottle from his pipe bowl against the post of the bunks. "But what about Gorraiz? Even if his head's okay, are we going to leave him here without a weapon? The rifle was stolen, remember?"

Jay realized that Vincent Gorraiz planned to move his flock farther, but there was probably no way he could move far enough or fast enough to avoid the wide-ranging riders from Wright's ranch, or whatever rancher had sent the night riders. They might even have been in the employ of the Cattlemen's Association, in which case no place in the Wyoming Territory would be a safe haven. Maybe Gorraiz knew this and that was why he was in no hurry. He was planning to stop right here, let his sheep crop the grass short and wait for his cousin to show up with his winter supplies. They couldn't leave the man alone and unarmed, with only a sheep dog for protection. For all the night riders knew, it was Gorraiz who had shot one of them from the dark last night. If they came back at all, it would be with blood in their eyes. Next time it wouldn't be just the sheep. Reluctantly, Jay had to concede that he and Hall would have to stay and give the man whatever protection they could and hope a posse from Rawlings or somewhere found them before anyone else did.

"Well?" Hall asked, as the silence stretched out between them.

"You're right," Jay finally said, nodding. "We can't leave him. We'll have to stay for now. Let's give it a day or two, and see what happens. Then, if we decide to go, we'll leave him one of our pistols and some ammunition. If he insists on staying here, there's not much we can do. We can't guard him from now on. Even if they attack again while we're here, I doubt if we can hold them off with two pistols among us."

"It's decided then," Hall agreed.

A loud, metallic ratcheting sound broke the stillness and Jay whirled toward the door, his hand halfway to his gun. A cocked Winchester was pointed at him around the edge of the door flap.

"The only thing's decided is that you two are coming with us," Bowlegs said, stepping into the room, holding the rifle.

Chapter Eighteen

Jay's heart sank as he caught movement out of the corner of his eye at the nearest window. Another man had thrown his leg over the sill of the other window and had a long-barrelled Colt trained on them.

Jay's hands went to shoulder level and stayed there. The would-be train robbers were back. He ground his teeth in frustration. What a fool he had been! Did he think these men would not return? They had shown up the first time during daylight; why not the second? A few minutes of inattention had been his undoing. Now, the three men surrounded them. Through the paneless window, Jay could see a fourth man outside, walking near Gorraiz, who still slept beneath a tree on his blanket. He wondered how these men had gotten so close to them without his hearing. They must have left their horses some distance off and walked up quietly on the flock so as not to startle the dog or the sheep. He had not heard Chuck bark, but either the dog had somehow been disabled or he just wasn't trained as a guard dog and did not set off an alarm at the sight of approaching strangers. Jay recalled that the dog had made no sound when they had walked into camp in the dark the first night with Gorraiz.

"What do you want?" Jay asked as the first man backed him toward the fireplace with the barrel of his rifle.

"Thought you were pretty clever, didn't ya?" the man sneered. "Flyin' off in that balloon like that."

The man was short and squatty and decidedly bowlegged, Jay noted.

"Figured after we peppered that balloon full of holes, you'd be coming down soon. Well, it took a little longer than we figured, but we gotcha now."

"What do you want?" Jay asked again. He scarcely dared look at the two sacks he had left lying by the chair when he had walked to the fireplace.

"I'll just take your gun. Slide it out real easy with two fingers and hand it over, slowly."

"The same goes for you," the second man said to Fletcher who also stood with his hands raised.

Jay did as he was instructed.

"Now, get over there with your pardner and turn around," Bowlegs ordered.

Jay experienced a moment of panic when he thought they were to be shot in the back. Sweat began to break out on his forehead and under his arms. He looked for some way to make a desperate break.

"Gotta make sure you don't have a hide-out knife or a Derringer up your sleeve."

Jay let out a breath in relief but kept his face a mask.

Bowlegs checked them both for hidden weapons and found only Jay's barlow knife, which he confiscated. He also took Hall's matches.

"Stand right where you are. Don't turn around."

Jay could hear the three men walking around the room.

"Well, what do we have here?" Bowlegs said. "Open those sacks," he commanded one of the others. Bowlegs was clearly the man in charge. "Dump it out on the table."

Jay heard a few seconds of scuffling.

"Damn, Jack, look at this! Stacks of bank notes and a pouch of gold coins. Must be worth thousands."

"Let me see."

Jay could hear someone pawing through the loot, and chanced a peek over his shoulder. All three men were grouped around the table, looking at the haul. No one was watching the prisoners. Bowlegs still held the rifle in his left hand, but he had let down the hammer on the weapon. The other two had holstered their pistols. He quickly gauged the distance to Bowlegs. If he could jump him and use him as a shield against the guns of the other two . . . but they would fire on Hall or the sheepherder.

Before he could decide anything, the moment was lost. One of the outlaws turned and read the look on his face.

"Don't try it, mister," he said, yanking his pistol. "He looked like he was about to jump you, Jack," the man said to Bowlegs. This outlaw was whip-thin and had a long, drooping mustache.

"Keep him covered," Jack Bowlegs replied absently as he continued raking through the contents of the sacks.

"Ah, here it is!" Jack held up the small, bamboo tube. He examined it carefully and then started to unwrap the brown paper from one end. The paper was torn and loose.

"This has been opened." He looked at Jay and Fletcher. "Who's been into this package?" he demanded, sharply.

Jay looked as blank as he was capable of looking. He glanced at Hall who took his cue and shrugged.

Jack Bowlegs pulled back the wrapping and shook the tube. Then he ran a finger inside and extracted the piece of paper, unfolded and read it. He glanced up at Jay, apparently attempting to hide the disappointment in his face. It was obvious to Jay that the cryptic note, "Palace Windsor Twelve Oaks" meant no more to this outlaw than it had to Jay and Hall. He folded the paper, put it back into the tube and carefully slipped the tube into his vest pocket.

"All right, let's go," he said, motioning with the rifle.

Jay and Hall moved toward the door.

"Jack, aren't we taking the money?" his coyote-faced companion asked, bewildered.

"No. Leave it. We got what we came for."

"But . . ."

"I said, leave it, Rafe!" Jack snapped. "The sheepherder can do whatever he wants with it. We're not taking it."

The third man grumbled something under his breath as he eyed the pile of loot. Rafe's hand reached out for the bag of gold coins.

Bowlegs swung on him with a snarl, shoving the Winchester muzzle under the man's chin.

"Are you hard of hearing?" The tone was deadly.

Fear and hate crossed Rafe's countenance as he slowly withdrew his hand and backed away out the door.

Jay and Fletcher followed him outside. Vincent Gorraiz was sitting up on his blanket, staring at the fourth man who was leaning casually against the big cottonwood, holding a Remington .44 loosely in one hand and smoking a cigarette.

"Let's go, you two," Jack Bowlegs said. "You can ride double on that mule."

"What do you want with us?" Jay asked. "You got what you wanted—whatever it was."

"I think our boss might want to talk to you."

"Who's your boss?"

"You'll find out."

"Why us?"

"I think one of you opened that package and looked at what was inside."

Jay shrugged. "Why would we do that? It was just . . ."

"Shut up and get on that mule!" Jack Bowlegs interrupted.

Jay went toward the hobbled mule with a sinking feeling in his stomach. He was thinking of another reason they were being taken along—they had seen the faces of the train robbers.

"You gonna steal this man's mule and leave him without a pack animal?" Hall asked.

"You just do as you're told and keep your mouth shut!" Coyote-face retorted, obviously still smarting from the rebuke by his leader.

Vincent Gorraiz did not look as if he had fully recovered. But he was alert to everything that was going on. He had gotten to his feet and watched in silence as Jay placed a hackamore with its lead rope on the mule and freed the animal from its hobbles. The man who had been guarding Gorraiz had gone to bring up the horses and, when he returned with them, they all mounted, Jay helping the aeronaut up behind him on the mule's bare back.

Jack Bowlegs led out, followed by Rafe Coyote-face, then the mule carrying double with the other two riders bringing up the rear. As Jay glanced back, Gorraiz gave him a silent thumbs-up sign. The gesture gave Jay a strange, comforting sensation as he turned back and settled in to follow wherever their captors were taking them. Somehow that signal told him Gorraiz understood and would not leave them to their fate. He didn't know what Gorraiz had in mind, but the sheepherder had kept silent through the whole ordeal. Gorraiz was a steady, cool head. And best of all, he knew this part of the country and the people who were both friend and foe. Jay began to look forward to whatever was coming with a ray of hope.

Chapter Nineteen

Jay estimated they rode about twelve miles, but it seemed much farther astraddle the bouncing backbone of the mule. The route followed the valley floor, winding around. Had they been able to ride cross-country, the distance would have been much shorter. Jay was able to keep track of the directions by the sun, but, if he had been asked to find his way back to the sheep camp, he would have been unable to do so without a lot of blundering around and guessing, and backtracking. The pace never slackened, and, by early afternoon, they reined up at a stout log ranchhouse facing out over a broad valley and with its back to a steeply-rising ridge that quickly climbed even higher into the mountains to the east.

"Get down," Bowlegs ordered after he had dismounted and tied his own chestnut to the hitching rail.

Fletcher Hall could hardly stand he was so stiff. Jay had shifted his weight to first one buttock and then the other as the mule had jolted along with a stiff-legged gait. This had minimized the effect, but he was still rather sore.

The four men herded them up onto the wooden porch and Bowlegs took off his hat before he rapped respectfully on the plank door. The place was a one-story, rambling type house with a shake roof, Jay noted as they waited for someone to answer the knock. He glanced at Hall, but the aeronaut's face was impassive as he stared straight ahead. He glanced quickly around. There was a pole corral off to one side, and he had seen a bunkhouse and a long barn as they rode up. He had noted a few hundred cattle grazing during the several-mile ride, but nowhere near the numbers he had expected, based on what Gorraiz had said about the range being overcrowded. But then, he remembered it took a lot more land to support one cow than it did back in Iowa or Illinois.

The door was jerked open abruptly by a spare, middle-aged woman in a plain dress. Her graying black hair was pulled back into a severe bun. Without a word she stood aside and motioned them in. The room was dark after the sunshine. The small, glassed windows that faced the porch admitted the only light. The back of the house was shut off by intervening rooms. The parlor was furnished with heavy, rudely made furniture, upholstered with horse blankets. No rugs covered the wide plank floor, and no curtains graced the windows. The only decoration on the walls was an old Sharps rifle hanging on a pair of polished buffalo horns. Nowhere was a woman's touch evident. Jay's confidence slipped a notch when all this was impressed on him in a matter of seconds. The six of them stood in the middle of the room while the woman disappeared down a hallway. In a few seconds she was back.

"Go on in the library." She pointed.

Jack Bowlegs and Rafe Coyote-face herded Jay and Hall toward the hallway, while the other two took this as their cue to leave by the front door.

Bowlegs lifted the wooden latch and pushed open the polished pine door. Jay and Hall followed, with Rafe bringing up the rear. Three walls of the room were lined with bookshelves from floor to ceiling. Seated behind a homemade wooden desk in a dark leather armchair was a tiny man with carefully slicked-down black hair, wearing gold, wire-rimmed spectacles. He was clean-shaven with a smooth, oval face.

"Shut the door," the man ordered, crisply. Rafe obeyed and then came to stand, hat in hand, before the desk with Jack. They seemed in awe of this small man.

"This is the Wells Fargo messenger and this is the aeronaut, Mr. Wright," Bowlegs said, pointing at each of them in turn.

"Did you get the message?" Wright snapped.

"Yes, sir, it's right here. It was with the stuff from the express box, just like you said it . . ."

His voice trailed off at the hard look Wright gave him, and he fumbled in a side pocket of his vest for the bamboo tube, handing it over quickly.

Wright glanced briefly at the address on the side and then slid a thin forefinger into the tube and extracted the paper. He unfolded and read it quickly, then smoothed the square of paper on the desktop and looked at it carefully. His face was a mask. He folded the paper and slipped it deftly back inside the tube.

"This has been opened," he stated flatly, staring at Bowlegs.

"It was like that when we found it, Mr. Wright," Jack hurriedly explained.

Jay suspected that the august Jacob Wright had no more idea what this cryptic note meant than anyone else did, but would not dare let his ignorance show in front of his own men. Jay had a sudden, irrational urge to laugh, but bit his cheeks to keep from it.

"Did you remove anything from this package?" Wright asked, fixing them with a hard stare.

"Nothing. That piece of paper was all there was," Jay answered. He hoped he sounded convincing.

Wright tapped one end of the small tube on his open palm, making a clicking sound with his mouth as he did so. Then he laid the tube on the desk and leaned back in his chair, carefully studying Jay and Hall for the first time. Jay noted that his eyes looked slightly larger through the lenses. This man looks less like a rancher than anyone I've ever seen, Jay thought as he stared back at the figure who sat with his small hands folded in his lap. His pale, olive complexion looked as if it had never seen the sun. He was wearing a soft, white cotton shirt and some sort of tan whipcord trousers. A large ledger lay closed on the desk by a green-shaded coal-oil lamp, but Wright had apparently been reading another book when they arrived, as a leather-bound volume lay closed in front of him, with a bookmark between its pages. Afternoon light, from the room's only window, flooded in behind him.

"Well, if you gentlemen are going to be my guests for a time, I suppose I should introduce myself. I am Jacob Wright, in case you didn't already know that. This is my ranch you are on, and I suppose you saw some of my cattle on your way here. They are scattered all around for miles."

Jay caught himself trying to anticipate what the man would say, and was preparing to defend himself and his companions concerning the flock of sheep, when the monologue took quite another direction.

"You have read the note in this container." It was a flat statement with no hint of friendliness in it.

Jay nodded.

"It is apparently in code. Can you tell me what it means?"

"No."

"Why did you open it?"

Jay and Hall looked sideways at each other. Jay did not know what was going on, but he was determined to be very careful with his answer. Jay had been in the habit of nearly always telling the truth, and the consequences be damned. As a result, he was not a convincing liar when he felt constrained to alter the truth. And lying to criminals did not seem wrong to him.

It was obvious Hall was not going to answer, so Jay shrugged and said, "I wanted to find out what we were carrying that train robbers would go to such great lengths to get."

"Were you not carrying a good deal of paper money and gold?" Wright asked, probing.

"Yes. But I would estimate it was not over thirty or forty thousand."

"And you do not think that amount of wealth worthy of great effort?"

Jay shook his head. "Possibly, but hardly likely. There are Wells Fargo express boxes on nearly every train. And there are banks and stages that still carry mine payrolls to places in Nevada . . ." He shrugged. "There are plenty of other opportunities for robberies that are easier and less risky. We had gotten away clean in that balloon. If they hadn't shot it full of holes, who knows? And then, when your men didn't take the money . . ."

"Ah, yes. Like shooting a deer and then following a trail of blood until he falls, exhausted. Easy pickings."

Wright got up and came around the desk. He was wearing knee-length, shiny riding boots. The flat heels were a good two inches thick, but still the man stood no more than five feet, three. He leaned his buttocks against the front edge of the desk and folded his arms.

"But you are right," he continued. "It was not the money. The few thousand you might be carrying was small change. And besides, it belongs to bankers and small investors, maybe a miner or rancher. I couldn't steal from them."

Strange morality, Jay thought. Apparently, dynamiting trains, shooting innocent people, and kidnapping were not on his list of forbidden actions.

Jay decided to take the initiative. "Well, now that you got that note, or whatever it is, we'll be on our way. It's a long ride back on that mule."

Jacob Wright allowed himself just the faintest trace of a smile. "Surely, Mr. McGraw, you are not as naive as that. You have seen my men robbing a train, shooting at you and others, stealing a package from Wells Fargo. Do you actually think I'm going to let you walk out of here? Hardly. There is much at stake here. I will do whatever I have to do."

A cold chill ran up Jay's back as he heard what amounted to his death sentence pronounced. But what really chilled him was the fact that this man knew his name. Jay McGraw's name had not been mentioned up to this point. He glanced at Fletcher Hall whose expression had not changed, but the color appeared to have drained from his florid complexion.

Jay swallowed hard and ran a hand across his forehead which was perspiring in spite of the cool air flowing into the room from the partially open window. He tried to keep his voice from shaking as he replied, "Then you won't mind telling us what all this is about."

Jacob Wright took a sheet of paper from the desk drawer and carefully printed a message on it in pencil. Then he folded it and gave it to Rafe Coyote-face. "Get this message to the telegraph office in Rawlings as fast as you can push a horse." Turning to Bowlegs, he said, "Wait in the parlor."

The two men departed, closing the door behind them.

Jacob Wright seated himself once again in the leather armchair, leaving Jay and Hall standing. Jay would have bet the partially open desk drawer contained a pistol.

"You may be surprised to learn that we also have Marvin Cutter in our custody."

Jay tried not to show any surprise. He didn't look at Hall.

"My men intercepted him not two miles from here. Apparently, he had taken off and left you to your own devices." He smiled faintly for the second time. "In fact, he told us where to find you—after a little persuasion."

Then his face grew solemn. "But I am digressing. Time is wasting. I am a man of business. First of all, since your lives are forfeit, I feel you at least deserve to know why you will be leaving this world shortly."

We won't go quietly, Jay was thinking, but his face revealed nothing as he stared at the cold black eyes of the diminutive rancher.

"You will remember the big robbery of the San Francisco mint some months ago," he began. "As you no doubt recall, about half of that gold was recovered, and our leader, Yen Ching, was sentenced to a long term in prison."

Jay must have visibly started, because Wright's eyes widened and he leaned forward slightly. "Oh, yes, Mr. McGraw, I know what part you played in capturing Yen Ching and finding those sacks of gold coins."

Jay's mind was racing. Wright had said, "our leader, Yen Ching." This man, then, was connected somehow to the huge tong leader from San Francisco who masterminded the great mint robbery to finance a revolution in China. And Wright also knew his, Jay's, role in solving the crime.

". . . seeking revenge," Wright was saying as Jay focused his attention once more. "I am told that you were initiated into the Chee Kong Tong and given the opportunity to help our cause by leading the men with the gold safely to Mexico, but you escaped and betrayed them. When you were brought into the tong, you swore an oath to never betray your brothers in the tong or your blood would soak the earth, no matter how far you ran or tried to hide. So you see that the arm of the tong is long and now we have you. And this time there will be no escape."

Jay felt Hall's curious glance on him. His mouth was dry and his knees weak, but he put on a bold front.

"Was all this trouble just to get me?" he demanded. "Hell, any tong member could have shot me down from ambush a hundred times in San Francisco."

"Don't flatter yourself, Mr. McGraw. You are only a tasty morsel in a much larger banquet." He pulled the middle desk drawer open farther, extracted a storekeeper's model Colt .45 and placed it on the desk top in front of him.

"That's just in case you have any insane idea of trying to overpower me and escape. I am small, but, I assure you, I am very quick and accurate with this. And, speaking of my size, you have no doubt noticed that I am not the robust outdoor type you might have expected in this rugged wilderness country. I am half Chinese. My father, Asa Wright, was a prospector who made a small stake and purchased a Chinese slave girl from San Francisco who became my mother. My father was not a bad man, but arrogant and overbearing, as most white men in this part of the country are. He could not have dealt with a woman who was his social equal. I think that is why he purchased a slave girl. But he left us after a few years and my mother brought me up in the traditions of her own people, and

I adopted their ways. We were very poor, and my mother worked hard to support us. But, when I was twelve, she contracted pneumonia in a Nevada mining camp and died, leaving me alone in the world. The white population shunned me as the skinny, weakling half-breed son of a slave girl, and for that I will always hate them. I worked, and stole my food when I had no work. I became very cunning and adept at the art of survival." He turned to stare blankly at the walls of books surrounding him, and was silent for a few seconds.

"Ah, but I digress again," he continued briskly. "Suffice it to say, I managed and grew up and acquired some measure of wealth and power in the white man's world. But my heart has always been with my mother's people, and with the suffering of the Chinese in their homeland. That is why I became affiliated with the Chee Kong Tong and supported Yen Ching's plan to take the white man's gold from the mint to finance a peasants' revolution in China against the Manchu rulers."

Maybe he is finally getting to the point of his story, Jay thought. He glanced sideways at Fletcher Hall whose expression clearly showed bewilderment at what he had gotten himself into.

"Even though half of that gold was recovered by the U.S. Government, we managed to conceal the rest of it—some million and a half dollars in double eagles—throughout Chinatown. But it was impossible for us to take it out because of the Law's close scrutiny of everyone coming and going from the Chinese quarter at that time. We finally made arrangements with a man whose bank was failing—a Mr. Julian Octavian Brown—to take the money for us and keep it until we could safely smuggle it out of the country. For a hefty fee, of course. You whites will do anything for money," he sneered, looking at Jay.

"You're half white yourself," Jay retorted. "Does that make you only half corrupt?"

For the first time, Jacob Wright showed some emotion. His face darkened and his hand reached for the gun on the desk. Behind the gold-rimmed glasses, pure hate shone from the hooded black eyes.

But he mastered himself with an obvious effort of will and slowly withdrew his hand and leaned back.

"The wealth of the world is like the tides of the world," he said. "It's never really gained or lost. It just ebbs and flows. At times there is a little more of it here and a little less of it there. My purpose is to direct more of it from the hands of the white hoarders to the cause of improving the lives of thousands of Chinese peasants. Gold—to pay for arms and soldiers to overthrow the Manchu dogs who have ruled my mother's people for more than two hundred years."

He took a deep breath and continued, "And, as I was saying, the banker agreed to take the money and keep it, for a price, until we deemed it safe to take it out of the country. We slipped it out of the Chinese quarter a little at a time after the searches were discontinued, and brought it to him. Two weeks ago, the tong leaders met and decided it was finally time to move the gold. But a strange thing happened. We had underestimated the greed of Mr. Brown. Instead of settling for his agreed fee, he decided he wanted to keep it all. He tried to stall, saying that the money had been invested and it would take time for him to collect it all again in gold. He tried to get us to accept his mining properties in Nevada in exchange for the gold we had entrusted to his care. Our leaders believed that he still had all the gold intact somewhere and was planning to abscond with the entire amount, leaving his bank to fail while he went to live in luxury in some remote paradise. So we sent the boo how doy, what you refer to as 'hatchet men,' to his estate to kidnap him and force him to reveal the whereabouts of the gold. Some of our boo how doy are very adept at wringing information from even the most recalcitrant of men. They have developed some ingenious, exquisite tortures that no human flesh can withstand. But, thanks to the warning of an old Chinese houseman, they were unable to take him by surprise, and by the time they had disposed of this servant, Brown had managed to write a note and slip it out by way of a boy who was working in his garden, and send the boy to the city on his fastest horse.

"By the time our men took Brown and learned that the note was bound for some business associate in Chicago, the message was already on its way. Then we wasted more time discovering that the message was going by Wells Fargo instead of the telegraph or the mail. To complicate things still further, your traveling companion, Marvin Cutter, notorious sneak thief, was on the grounds, apparently attempting to steal from Brown, and witnessed one of the boo how doy split the skull of the Chinese houseman and grab Mr. Julian O. Brown.

"Cutter managed to elude us, but the tong found out a few hours later that he had been jailed for picking pockets. One of our best men was sent to silence him in jail, only to discover that he had escaped about two hours earlier and vanished. Now we know, of course, where he went, don't we?"

He allowed himself one of those smiles that did not touch his eyes and was as mirthless as the grin of a jackal.

"If I believed in a power higher than myself, I would have to say that some god had arranged all this. We have Cutter, we have the note, albeit in code, telling us of the gold, and we have you, who have grievously betrayed your blood brothers. It has all come together in such a neat package."

"I was forced to go through that ridiculous initiation ceremony into the tong when I was a captive," Jay said, irritably.

"No matter."

"Why do you need this note decoded? Why don't your hatchet men, who are so expert at torture, just force the information from Brown?" Jay asked. His fear had been dulled by strain, fatigue, and lack of sleep. For the moment he just wanted to fasten his mind on this puzzle—a puzzle that had been getting more complex since Cutter had shown up in his express car. His tired brain still saw some missing pieces, and since there was no hope of escaping here and now, he let his curiosity have free rein.

"There was a slight problem with that," Wright answered. "One of our men got a little over-enthusiastic and Mr. Brown died. Of course, that man paid with his life for so drastic a mistake. But, nevertheless, it left us with only this note to give us a clue as to the location of the million and a half in gold."

"What about the man in Chicago the note is addressed to?"

"I have dispatched a rider to the Western Union office in Rawlings with a message to our brothers in Chicago to lay hands on this man, if he can be found. But we have no assurance that he can decipher this note either."

"What makes you think this note has any reference to gold at all?" Jay asked.

Jacob Wright eyed him through the magnifying lenses. "Maybe that is the reason you are only a Wells Fargo messenger. Of course, you are very young yet. If you were destined to live longer, you might learn more about the nature of men and their motives. If a man who has stolen much gold sees or hears his captors, torturers, or executioners coming for him in his house, and he has only a few minutes before they arrive, what do you suppose would be his last act?"

"If I couldn't get away, I'd pray."

"Not if your whole life centered around this huge amount of gold, as Brown's did. No. His last desperate act before the hatchet men found him in his study and chopped through the door would be to somehow get a note outside to a friend telling where the gold was hidden. And this he did by way of the boy in the garden just outside his window. I don't know of this Simpson fellow, but I'll wager we find that he is a business partner or a banking associate of Brown's who is aware of the tong's deal with Brown."

"Then if this Simpson doesn't know the meaning of the note, you are as far away from the gold as ever," Jay said. He wanted to gloat, but he was too tired and too scared. He just wanted to sit down somewhere and close his eyes for a nap.

"We will break the code," Wright said confidently. "The authorities do not yet know that Brown is dead. And they have no reason to connect the tong with his disappearance."

Oh yes they do, Jay thought, recalling Fred Casey's mentioning the tong trademark of the Chinese houseman's skull being split. But he kept silent.

"A telegraph message will be sent to San Francisco with the words of this note as soon as one of my men can reach Rawlings," Wright continued. "In the meantime, I hope I have satisfied all your curiosity concerning this matter. I like things tied up in nice, neat packages, and I would hate for a man to enter the black void not understanding all the reasons for his going."

"Robbing that train has already put the law on your trail," Jay retorted. "And killing us will definitely increase that to a hanging offense."

"Oh, I don't plan to kill you and your friends," Wright said, brightly. "We will arrange for a little accident. It will be an accident that could happen to anyone such as yourselves not familiar with these mountains." He made a tent of his fingers and touched them to his pursed lips. "I would tell you what to expect, but I don't want to ruin all your surprises."

He picked up the loaded Colt and got up, stepping around the desk. His movements were all small and precise.

"If you gentlemen will open that door behind you, we'll be on our way."

Chapter Twenty

When Jay awoke some hours later, he had no idea what day it was, and only the vaguest recollections of what had been happening to him. And he was terribly thirsty.

He pushed himself up to a sitting position from the bare dirt floor of what appeared to be a log woodshed and rubbed the sleep from his gritty eyes. In the dim light that filtered between the unchinked logs of the walls, he saw Fletcher Hall sitting on the floor a few feet away, watching him. Heavy, steady breathing sounded on the other side where Marvin Cutter lay, close to the base of the wall, head pillowed on his arm, and fast asleep. He looked even grimier and more unkempt than Jay remembered him.

"You been asleep a long time," Hall remarked. His own red, puffy eyes told a tale of sleeplessness.

"What time is it?"

Hall consulted his watch. "About six-fifteen."

Jay was confused. He felt as if he had slept more than two or three hours. "Six-fifteen?"

"In the morning. You been asleep more than twelve hours."

"Where are we?" Try as he might, he could not remember the details of anything that had transpired after the meeting with Jacob Wright.

"We're only about fifty yards from the ranchhouse. Old Bowlegs brought us here and locked us in around four o'clock yesterday afternoon. Appears to be some sort of woodshed." He gestured at the inside of their prison, and Jay looked around at the split lengths of firewood stacked loosely in two corners of the eight by ten foot pine log structure. No fresh wood had been thrown in here for some time, and cobwebs festooned most of the corners. The place smelled musty and unused. It was about time for someone to lay in a fresh supply of winter firewood, Jay noted absently.

He ran a hand over his face and combed his fingers through his hair. "I was dead on my feet. Didn't realize how tired I was. You don't look like you slept too well, though."

"Got a few catnaps in is all," Hall replied. "Kept waking up with nightmares. Don't know how you can sleep so soundly, considering what's going on here."

Jay nodded as he got stiffly to his feet. "If that half-breed Chinese fellow has his way, we'll all be sleeping pretty soundly before long."

"I don't know how you can be so flippant about it," Hall growled, turning away and placing his eyes to a crack between the logs.

"Have to keep my spirits up. We're not dead yet."

Hall turned a haggard face toward him. "Got any ideas how to get out of here?"

Jay looked around at the log structure. The heavy sleep had left him feeling somewhat dull and lethargic. But he knew that would pass shortly. His youthful strength and energy were back. He knew a little food would bring him back to his peak. Even though he had not eaten in twenty-four hours, he was not hungry. Only thirsty. Hall was a different story. Even though the man was stocky and strong, he was probably fifteen or twenty years older than Jay, and unused to hardships of losing sleep and going without food. Jay wondered about his physical stamina. If there was an opportunity for a breakout, would Hall have the speed and endurance to take advantage of it? Or would Jay have to wait for him and for Cutter? Living by his wits on the streets had probably conditioned the thief for nearly anything. In any case, Jay resolved not to worry too much about him.

"Have you checked the door?" Jay asked. Might as well start with the obvious.

"First thing. Solid pine planks about three inches thick. I heard them drop a bar in place across it."

"Huh. Evidently they use this place for things other than just to store firewood."

Jay walked around, inspecting the corners. The logs were notched and fit closely. A little air and a little daylight could get through the cracks, but that was all, except maybe a fieldmouse. The ceiling was supported by squared-off pine logs, crossed with small pine or cedar poles and topped with some type of wooden shakes. The flat roof was canted slightly from back to front to allow runoff. The supporting beams were about seven feet up. Maybe if he could climb up a pile of wood in the corner and reach it, he could use a hunk of firewood to batter a hole in the roof. But, because of the noise, this would have to be done when nobody was at the house. Had Wright left a guard? There was very likely someone close by who could keep an eye on the place, and maybe a closer guard at night. And night was many hours away.

"Well?" Hall asked.

"We might be able to knock a hole in that roof if we had plenty of time and nobody could hear the noise we would make. It would sure help if we knew what they planned to do with us. Did he mention anything about how long we have?"

Hall shook his head. "Nothing. Just had Bowlegs bring us down here and lock us in."

"Do you think if Wright thought we knew what that note meant, he'd keep us alive until we told him?"

"No. If he thought we knew, we'd be tortured. And for what purpose? We don't."

"We could tell him anything."

"He'd hold us until he found out it was a lie, and then kill us."

"It might buy us some time," Jay mused. "There has to be a posse combing these hills, looking for us by now. They've probably even found our balloon, who knows?"

Hall nodded. "Yeah, who knows? But we can't rely on that. We have to make some plans to defend ourselves now."

"Well, they won't walk in here and shoot us down, anyway. Wright said he was arranging some sort of 'accident.' My guess is that it will be out away from this ranchhouse. Maybe somewhere in the mountains. Wright wouldn't take a chance on our bodies being found near here."

"Huh! Hope you're right," Hall grunted. "Of course he could always kill us here and haul our bodies somewhere else and dump them."

128

The same thought had occurred to Jay, but he was forcing himself to put the best light on things. It wouldn't do to start getting depressed and lose hope now. If only they knew what "surprise" Wright had in store for them!

Marvin Cutter began to stir, then sat up, blinking and rubbing the sleep from his eyes with a fist.

"Morning, gents," he greeted them, showing a yellow-toothed grin through the long black stubble on his lean cheeks. "It *is* morning, isn't it?" he asked, squinting at the slats of oblique light striping them from between the pine logs. "Yeah, I reckon it is," he said, nervously glancing at the two men standing above him. "What's for breakfast?" he asked, pushing himself erect by means of the log wall behind him.

"How's the knee?" Jay asked.

"Oh, much better," he answered hurriedly, ignoring the sarcasm.

"I'll bet it's much better than Vincent Gorraiz's head."

"Oh, that. I really didn't mean to hit him so hard. Fact is, I was trying to slip out of there quietly, but I saw him on guard, and knew I wouldn't get a half-mile if I didn't put him out for a while. But I'm not a violent man, you know."

"A bunch of cowboys showed up right after you left and started shooting up the flock," Hall added. "Did you see or hear any of that?"

"So that's what that shooting was about. I just could hear it. I musta been more than a mile away by then."

"Nice of you to come back and help out," Jay said.

Cutter shrugged. "Say . . . I heard the two men who brought me here talking about one of the hands being shot. They didn't say what happened, but they had him in the bunkhouse and were going to take him by wagon to Rawlings to the doctor. Musta been hit pretty bad, 'cause they were wonderin' if he could stand the trip."

Jay and Fletcher looked at each other.

"Likely the one we got," Hall said.

"Did you overhear anything else?" Jay asked. "Anything about what else might be going on around here?"

Cutter shook his head.

"Did you meet Jacob Wright?" Jay asked.

"Who?"

"The owner of this ranch."

"Oh, him. Yeh. Strange-looking little fella."

"Then you know they're going to kill you," Jay said.

Cutter swallowed hard and looked away.

"Why didn't you tell us you were running from the tong? It might have saved us all from this."

"I didn't want to be mixed up in any of this," Cutter said in a low voice, still not looking at Jay.

"Well, you're in it and so are we."

"Why in hell didn't you at least tell us what that note meant?" Hall demanded angrily.

"I don't know what it means," Cutter whined defensively. "I just recognized the handwriting, is all."

"But you were there at his estate—in his house—when he wrote it," Jay persisted. "You saw the hatchet men chop down that poor Chinese servant."

Cutter nodded, dumbly.

"What were you doing at Julian Octavian Brown's estate?"

Cutter took a deep breath and let it out in a rush. "Okay, okay, I'll tell you the whole story. I don't suppose it matters now." He paused and ran his fingers through his hair that was matted with dirt and twigs. "Julian Brown met me on the street about fifteen years ago. In fact, I had just pinched his billfold as he was coming out of the Palace Hotel. I didn't know who he was, but he looked like he had a lot of money, from the way he was dressed. Well, one of the men with him seen me do it, and grabbed me before I could get away. Well, to make a long story short, the old man felt sorry for me and didn't turn me in to the police. I seen that he kinda wanted to take me under his wing, not having any children of his own, so I give him a sad story about my upbringing—which wasn't all that joyous, as you can probably understand. Anyhow, he offered me a job on his estate and I took it. Worked in his stables and just did whatever jobs needed doin' around there for several months. Well, these hands were never made to fit a shovel and directly, I'd had enough of that, so I lit out. The old man was kind enough to me and fed me well, so I didn't relieve him of none of his valuables when I left—and God knows, there was stuff laying around everywhere that I could've picked up and sold for cash. Well, anyways, I'd run into him on the street now and then, but he never said anything to me or I to him. We just went our separate ways. I reckon he just considered it an experiment that failed.

"Well, a month or two ago, things started getting really tough on the street. More competition, if you know what I mean. Lots of people out of work. And I got beat up a couple of times when I picked on the wrong man. I guess my hands were shaky from being hung over. Anyway, it got to the point where I almost had to get caught so I could get put in jail to have a place to sleep and something to eat. Well, I finally decided I'd go out to Brown's estate and see if I could come up with something valuable that was small enough to carry off that I could sell to keep me going for a few months. As I said, things were really getting difficult on the streets, and the police were getting harder on us. They'd just as soon whip me with a nightstick as run me in. I walked the ten miles to Brown's place, since I had no money. I was familiar with the layout so it was no trouble for me to get into the grounds at night without being seen. Slept in the stable when I couldn't find anything outside to cart off.

"Figured I'd slip into the house come daylight after the old man had gone off to the city in his carriage and see if there was some gold trinket he wouldn't even miss. As it turned out, I didn't know the old man didn't go to his bank every day, and when he didn't come out the next morning, I figured maybe he wasn't even home, so I went in through the back servant's entrance. Before I could even work my way back to the study, I heard someone coming so I jumped into the pantry that was handy. It was the Chinese houseman.

"I heard him shout something in Chinese and there was a crashing of glass and the old servant went running past the pantry, yelling for Mr. Brown to run for his life. Then these other Chinese came bustin' in and went for the old man and then I didn't hear any more except some scufflin' around down the hall in another part of the house, then a couple of shouts. When I took a peek outside of the pantry, there was the houseman on the floor in the doorway to the kitchen with his head split open. It about made me sick. There was blood everywhere. I knew I had to get out of there, 'cause I figured they had killed Brown, too. But, as luck would have it, they saw me slipping out the back door and raised a helluva shout. I guess the only thing that saved me was that I was really scared and could run faster. And they were distracted by the young fella who was a gardener taking off on a fast horse toward the road. I knew the grounds and I managed to dodge them and get over the wall and into the trees and hide until they were gone. I stayed there all day and then walked back to town after dark. I can tell you I jumped at every sound on the way, too. But I knew they had seen me, and I had seen them. They knew I could tell the police and describe them, so I knew I had to get myself put in jail for safety. That's why I let myself get caught filching billfolds at that balloon demonstration the next day.

"But even after I got jailed, I was afraid there were ways the tong could get me. Well, I watched for a chance to escape. I been in and out of that jail so much over the past few years that all the jailers know me. I'm like one of the family. Because of that, I guess, they got a little careless. I'm good with my hands and, when the night shift came on duty and brought me my supper, I filched the cell key and stashed it under my mattress until things got quiet, and the turnkey had settled down to doze in his chair; then I was out of there and gone as fast and quiet as a cat. I hid out in an old, empty building until daylight, then lifted a few dollars from a well-dressed gentleman who wouldn't miss it, and grabbed the ferry over to Oakland and stowed away on the first eastbound train I saw."

Jay let out a sigh as if he had been doing all the talking and was out of breath. "That pretty well clears up the mystery, except that nobody seems to know where the gold is."

"To hell with the gold," Hall said. "What about us?"

No more the dapper, cocky aeronaut who thrilled crowds with his derring-do. He had been reduced to a scruffy, middle-aged man fearful for his life.

"If we have to make a quick break for it, do you feel up to it?" Jay asked.

Hall nodded. "Just give me a chance."

Jay went to the wall and peeked out through one of the larger cracks. "No sign of life around the house." He pulled out the watch that had not been taken from him. "Six-thirty. If this were really a working ranch, don't you think we'd see somebody up and around by now?"

"Not necessarily," Hall replied. One or two of them may have taken the wounded cowboy to Rawlings. Another one—Coyote-face—was sent in to Rawlings with that message to the Western Union office. Remember? If there are any others working on this place they may have been sent after Vincent Gorraiz."

"I hope he had enough sense to move his flock on farther away or back up into the mountain meadows for now."

Hall nodded. "Me, too. And I guess Wright and that woman who opened the door are probably inside the house."

"Then, if there's nobody within earshot, I'll have a try at this ceiling," Jay said.

He climbed up the pile of loose firewood in the corner, picking up a thick piece of pine about two feet long as he went. A mouse scuttled out of the pile and darted under the bottom log of the wall. Jay wiped a sleeve across his face to clear the spiderwebs wrapped around his head. Selecting a likely spot, he pounded the pine log into the ceiling two, three times with all the strength in his arms. It felt solid. He forced the end of the log upward several more times like a battering ram, then stopped to catch his breath and rest. If there was any weak spot in this ceiling, this wasn't it. He looked around. He saw no gaps or chinks or rotten spots.

While he was still staring upward, a shot exploded and a bullet slammed into the top log of the wall near his head. He staggered back and fell down the sloping woodpile on his back, with a raucous laugh echoing in his ears.

A rifle barrel was being withdrawn from between the wall logs at the far end of the shed.

"Let's not be destroyin' Mr. Wright's property in there," Jack Bowlegs' voice said. The laugh receded as Bowlegs moved away.

"You okay?" Hall asked, getting up and brushing himself off. Cutter still cowered against the wall.

"Yeah. Just startled me," Jay answered, rolling off the woodpile. "So much for that idea. Wright left his favorite guard dog on duty."

The three of them stood and looked at each other as the narrow strips of sunlight illuminated the swirls of acrid powder smoke that eddied about the room. The smell was as bitter as their outlook for the rest of this day— possibly their last day on earth.

Chapter Twenty-One

The sun was slanting down in the western sky when there was a thump at the door and it swung outward. Bowlegs stood there, hat square on his head, holding Gorraiz's Winchester on them. "Time to go, gents."

The three of them moved outside into the fresh, cool air. Wright, dressed in a black suit and hat and a white shirt, was sitting on the front seat of a wagon, staring down at them through his gold-rimmed glasses.

"Climb aboard." Bowlegs gestured with the rifle.

They silently got up into the rear seat of the high-wheeled wagon.

"Mind if I have a drink of water before we go?" Jay asked.

"Help yourself," Wright said, pointing at the wooden rain barrel that stood full under a corner eave of the house. "But don't make any sudden moves," he called after them as all three jumped down and made for the water.

Jay swept off the collection of fallen leaves and small water spiders that covered the surface and then took a long drink of the cool water. When Hall and Cutter had finished their turns, Jay splashed some of the water on his face and hair. He felt greatly refreshed.

As they climbed back into the wagon, Jay noticed that Wright was holding his storekeeper's model Colt in his lap. Bowlegs took the reins and slapped the team of Morgans into motion.

Wright turned to hang over the back of the seat, his pistol held loosely in one hand.

"Would it be too much to ask where we're going?" Jay inquired.

"You'll find out soon enough."

"I'm surprised you haven't got us all tied up," Jay continued, trying to goad the rancher.

"No sense in doing that. If you tried to jump off and run, we'd gun you down before you got twenty yards. Besides, if we happened to run into a posse, we could always say we found you wandering in the mountains and were taking you into Rawlings. It would be our word against yours."

"Vincent Gorraiz would swear to what really happened."

"Who? Oh, the sheepherder. Yes. Well, we'll be dealing with him tonight. Anyone who doesn't have the sense to run in the face of such overwhelming odds deserves to be squashed like a bug. In fact, should your bodies ever be found, and any foul play is suspected, I can always put out the rumor that you were mistaken for sheep men who just got caught up in this nasty range war. How was anyone to know you were from the train? After all, you were traveling with a Basque sheepherder."

The wheels jolted in and out of a rut that had dried in a low wash.

"You actually run a cattle ranch here, or is this just a front for all your other activities?" Jay asked.

"Oh, I assure you, this is a legitimate cattle ranch. But I never miss a chance to do what I can to further the aims of my tong. But I was particularly incensed to discover that about half the gold from the mint was recovered, thanks to you and that Secret Service agent and that policeman friend of yours—what was his name?"

"Fred Casey," Jay said.

"Ah yes, Casey. Our men in San Francisco will be dealing with him shortly also. No one gets away with trying to thwart the Chee Kong Tong and lives long afterward. Still and all, even though we lost half the gold, a million and a half will give us a good start on equipping a revolutionary army."

The diminutive rancher seemed to be in an expansive mood, so Jay tried drawing him out on a more immediate subject.

"What do you plan to do with us?"

Again, that mirthless smile played about his thin lips. "I don't want to spoil your surprise. We should be there in less than a half-hour." Still keeping one eye on his passengers, he slipped a gold watch from his vest pocket and glanced at it. Then he cast a look at the sun that was sliding down the slope of the western sky toward the horizon of low hills.

"Ah, just right."

The team was pulling the wagon at a trot on a faint, two-wheel track of road that was going in a generally northwest direction, winding through the foothills of the Sierra Madre Range. It was a beautiful autumn evening, and Jay felt rested and strong, but slightly light-headed from not having eaten anything in about thirty-six hours. His body was low on fuel, yet he felt he still had some reserves to call on, if needed. He had no sensation of hunger, but knew that if he were not under such mental stress, his lean stomach would be growling for food.

Bowlegs slowed the team and then pulled them into a tight turn off the road, angling upward through some widely-spaced pines and fir. Another ten minutes of weaving back and forth through the conifers that continued to grow thicker, brought them to an impassable mass of boulders and ledges of rock and fallen timber.

"We have to walk from here," Wright said, hopping lightly down, and holding his gun steady on them.

The three climbed down and began walking ahead of the rancher's leveled Colt. Jay saw Bowlegs tie the team to a fallen limb and follow them with the rifle. Jay noted that Jack Bowlegs had picked up the loose coils of a new hemp rope from under the wagon's seat and carried it over his free arm. The thought crossed Jay's mind that they were to be hanged, and his throat constricted at the horrible image this conjured up. If they were found, their deaths could very well be attributed to the range war. But then, hadn't Wright said their deaths were to look like an accident? Jay silently resolved that if hanging was to be their fate, he would make a break for it. To his way of thinking, being shot was preferable to choking out his life at the end of a rope.

Another ten minutes or so of walking brought them suddenly out of the dense pine forest almost to the edge of a sheer cliff.

They halted and Jay's eyes darted around, looking for an opportunity to make a break. He wasn't about to wait to be forced over the edge of a cliff to his death.

But, apparently that was not what Wright had in mind, either. The black-suited rancher nodded to Bowlegs who handed his rifle to Wright. Wright holstered his Colt and backed away a few steps, holding the rifle waist high, covering them.

Bowlegs whipped the end of the rope around a nearby pine that was about two feet in diameter at its base, deftly threw a bowline into it, and yanked it a couple of times to be sure it was tight. Then he flung the coils of rope over the edge of the precipice.

"There's a cave in the side of this cliff about thirty feet down," Wright said. "Grab that rope and slide yourselves down into it."

So that was it, Jay thought. They were to be marooned to die of hunger and thirst in some inaccessible cave where their yells for help would go unheard. He looked out and saw the cliff edge faced the west, and the setting sun. Looking down, he saw a talus slope about two hundred feet below that sloped off into a heavy stand of fir trees. Beyond that were the gently rolling hills and intervening valleys by which they had ascended to this ridge. The ranchhouse was somewhere out of sight to his left, Jay guessed, maybe two or three miles away.

"Step lively, gentlemen! I must get home before dark!" Wright said, crisply. "You first." He jabbed the gun at Cutter.

"No, no. Don't make me go," he wailed, taking a step toward Wright. "Please. I'll work for you. You know I'm not with them," he whined, motioning toward McGraw and Hall.

Jay heard genuine fear in the panicky voice.

"I'll do anything you want. Please! Just don't put me over that edge." He dropped to his knees in front of Wright, sniveling.

In spite of his own fear, Jay was embarrassed for the thief.

Wright seemed startled at first, but quickly regained his composure. "Get away from me, you useless piece of dung," he almost sneered. "Take hold of that rope or Jack will throw you over."

Cutter, looking like a man ascending the scaffold, picked up the rope and, backing carefully to the edge, felt with his slick-soled shoes for some sort of footing and went over the lip. The rope grew taut as he walked himself down the cliff face and out of sight. After a couple of minutes, the rope grew slack.

"Next!"

Hall glanced at Jay and then picked up the rope and proceeded to follow. Hall slipped the rope under one leg to take some of the strain off his arms and expertly rappelled himself over the edge.

Wright's eyes were positively glowing with delight, Jay thought as he glanced at the rancher.

"And, last but not least, Mr. McGraw!" Wright announced with a flourish.

Jay could see no immediate chance of escape, so he grasped the rope and eased himself over the edge after his companions.

The last thing he saw as he went down was the small rancher holding the rifle on him, and the impassive face of Bowlegs as he stood by the tree with his hand on the rope and the westering sun glinting off the silver conchos on his leather vest.

Then, all his concentration lay on getting safely down into the cave. Once, his shoes slipped as some loose rock rolled under them and his body swung in against the cliff face, jarring the wind from his chest. But he again planted his shoe soles and pushed back, letting the rope slide slowly as he walked backward down the sheer face. He didn't look down; he only felt with his feet. It seemed as if he was never going to reach it, but he steadfastly kept his eyes dead ahead, seeing only the weathered granite slowly slide past.

Finally, his probing feet found nothing and he grunted as his shins scraped sharp rock. He hung on his arms and let himself down hand over hand another half a body length. Then there were hands grasping him and easing him into the declivity and down to the slanting cave floor. As soon as he let go of the rope, it began to jiggle and dance as Bowlegs pulled it back up. On an impulse, Jay reached out for the rope that was fast rising in front of him, grabbed it with both hands and threw all his weight on it in one motion. He felt a heavy tug at the other end, like a huge fish on a line. Then came a muffled curse. He yanked hard again, pulling a few feet of the line inside the cave. But the element of surprise was gone now. They would not see the startled cowboy hurtling past them to his death on the rocks below.

"Might as well quit playing tug-o'war with him," Hall said. "They've got us."

After his first mighty jerk, Jay also realized the futility of it, and now let it drop, feeling the slight friction burns on his hands.

The rope vanished upward and then there was silence. There was no conversation from above, nor did they hear the men leave. The three of them looked at each other. They had been placed in a niche on the wall of the mountain, and left to die of starvation and thirst. Jay had a sinking feeling in the pit of his stomach.

With nothing better to do, he used the last rays of the setting sun that were slanting into the mouth of the cave, to examine their prison. The cave itself was only about twenty feet deep and about twice as long, its slightly uneven floor from side to side, slanting at about a thirty-degree angle. It had apparently been carved by wind and water action on the face of the granite cliff. When Jay lay on his belly and thrust his head out, looking up and down, he could see the whole upthrust stratum of granite ran diagonally. The talus slope was still a good hundred and fifty feet below. It would take an expert mountain climber with plenty of gear to scale or descend that rock face, he thought, withdrawing his head and pushing himself to his feet.

Here and there on some of the seams of the weathered rock face, a few small evergreens had somehow found enough nourishment to take root. Unfortunately, they were out of reach from the cave, and were too widely spaced to help. Jay wondered if they were deeply rooted enough to hold a grown man's weight even if they had a rope. Idle speculation, he concluded. Of more immediate concern was finding food and water. Hall and Cutter were also silently examining their new home—with looks of dismay on their faces.

The roof of the cave at its mouth was about ten feet high, but it sloped down quickly to meet the floor at the back, maybe twenty-five feet at its deepest, Jay estimated. Where the ceiling met the floor was a crack about four inches high and roughly ten feet long. Jay got down on his hands and knees and examined it. No cool air issued from it. Apparently it didn't go anywhere. There was only one heartening thing about this crack. Water had seeped out of it and run down to the lower end of the cave floor where it had collected in a pool. However, that pool was dry now. Only a little damp moss and a trace of mud remained. Evidently, water seeped through this layered rock in rainy weather, but it had not rained lately. The dry autumn season was upon them. And Jay suspected, from the size of the seepage, they would all be long dead before enough water collected here to sustain the three of them.

He straightened up and looked around, feeling as hopeless as he ever had in his entire life. They were marooned without food, water, blankets, matches, fuel, or weapons. If he had known what was coming, he would have made a break for it earlier. A quick bullet would have been preferable to a slow death from exposure and starvation. But he had held off, assuming he would have a better opportunity to escape. But not even an aeronaut like Hall could escape from this place without wings. It was more secure than the Tower of London. He ground his teeth and swore softly to himself in frustration.

The floor of the cave was covered in soft dust, apparently blown in from somewhere outside. There were no marks in this dust and no sign of black smoke on the ceiling to indicate that fire-making humans had ever occupied this place, even briefly. But that was understandable, since, except by rope ladder from above, it was completely inaccessible.

One thing Jay did notice before their own walking around obliterated them was some tiny, wavy ridges in the dust from the upper end of the cave to the back. Some quirk of the wind had ridged the dust like tiny, wind-made sand dunes, he guessed.

One five-foot cedar tree was growing in the scant soil, its roots clinging precariously to the cracked rock just at the upper end of the cave, but there was hardly enough wood in this tree for one campfire—even if they had any matches, a knife or a hatchet, which none of them did.

They were all lost in their own thoughts, gloomily assessing their chances of survival. No one spoke as the sun settled and shadow crept into the cave along with the first cool air of the evening chill to follow. A fire might attract someone's attention at night, if the light could be seen from the road they had come up on. Maybe if they could get a fire going by stripping off some of the small, resinous limbs of the cedar with their hands and striking a piece of granite and steel . . . Jay's thought trailed off into hopelessness. They had no steel, unless one of them had something metallic in his pocket. As for tinder, maybe some threads from their clothing would be flammable enough. None of them wore spectacles. The magnifying eyeglasses of Wright would be perfect for focusing the rays of the sun and starting a fire. But they had none.

Finally, the gloomy atmosphere was settling in deeper than twilight, and Jay felt he had to take the lead and say something to dispel the mood.

"Hell, boys, we aren't whipped yet. We'll figure a way out of this." His words sounded hollow, even to himself. They didn't reply. He tried again. "If we put our heads together, we can come up with something."

He walked over toward the lone cedar to inspect it a little closer. He had already resolved in his own mind to make an attempt at climbing down, or up, the rock face before he became too weakened by hunger and thirst to try it. And he had already gone almost two days without food. He couldn't wait much longer.

Just as he reached for the cedar, he caught a movement out of the corner of his eye at the base of the tree and leapt back, startled. His heart was pounding as he instinctively reached for the Colt that was not there. Then, in the shadows of the mountain cave he saw it, and knew what the wavy marks in the dust meant. At the same time he heard a noise like the wind rattling dry reeds as the rattlesnake reacted to his presence and threw himself into a coil, the upright tail buzzing its warning.

"Oh, damn!" Cutter breathed behind him.

Jay froze with fear. His legs felt paralyzed. He willed himself to move, but his body would not respond. Other rattlesnakes were gliding past the first. Two of them, sensing the human body heat, coiled, tails buzzing, forked tongues flicking in and out, heads drawn back to strike. Other reptilian forms slithered toward the crack at the back of the cave.

With the dying of the warm sunlight they were returning to their underground shelter. Probably getting ready to den up for the winter, Jay thought. But the thought was no comfort as the night came down and the deadly buzzing continued only a few feet away.

Chapter Twenty-Two

Jay forced down the panic as he stared into those slitted eyes that were fixed on him. "Move away—slowly," he said finally regaining control of his legs and stepping softly backward. He had always heard that a rattlesnake could strike twice the length of its body, and he estimated this one to be more than five feet long and as big around as his arm. Its venom would be deadly.

Cautiously, gradually, he retreated, watching the poised head, and ready to spring aside if it struck, knowing that he probably would not be quick enough. Out of the corner of his eye he could see Fletcher Hall and Marvin Cutter moving carefully back toward the lower end of the short cave.

When he knew he was out of range, his breath escaped in an involuntary rush.

"If we stay down here at the far end and don't move, they'll probably go on about their business," Hall whispered hoarsely.

"Their business might be having us for supper," Cutter replied.

But Hall was right. In a few minutes, the big rattlers, one by one, dropped out of their defensive coils. Jay shivered at the whispering sounds of their bodies moving across the fine sand and dust of the rock floor toward their lair somewhere beyond the crack that opened into the base of the back wall.

"Wish I had some matches," Hall said. "Fire would keep them at bay."

"As long as they don't perceive us as a threat, we should be all right," Jay said.

"Wonder how we let 'em know that," Cutter snickered nervously.

"First good cold snap will probably send them underground for the winter," Jay continued in a low voice. "But as long as the sun is warm during the day, they'll be out sunning themselves."

"In the meantime, we share this cave with them," Cutter said. "That's comforting. I wonder if that little half-breed knew they were here."

"I'm sure he did. That's probably one reason we're here. This is something that would appeal to his twisted sense of humor."

The last of the snakes disappeared into the crack and the three men sat down on the sloping floor to rest as the twilight deepened into darkness.

"Wish I had some matches," Hall said again, sucking on his empty pipe. "Got a little tobacco left, but they took my matches when they took my gun and my penknife."

Eyeing the crack at the back of the cave to be sure the reptiles were gone for the time being, Jay walked to the upper end of the cave and carefully pushed aside the branches of the small cedar tree. The light was dying but he carefully studied the cliff face where the cave opening narrowed back into it. The upthrust of the ancient rock had been at the same angle as the cave—about thirty degrees. Erosion had either created or enlarged this cave, and the same forces of wind and water were still at work on the cliff face. The runoff from above, the water seeping between the layers of rock, the expanding and contracting forces of frost, had grooved the rock layers, forming larger cracks.

After a good ten minutes, he returned to his companions.

"Whatcha looking at?"

"Those snakes had to come from somewhere," Jay replied. "They didn't fly up or down here. There's a narrow ledge leading from the upper end of this cave. A man would have to turn his feet sideways and press flat against the cliff to walk on it. It goes up and out about twenty or thirty feet and then I can't see any farther because of a bulge in the wall."

"You thinking about trying it?" Cutter asked.

Jay didn't reply for a moment. Then he said, "I might." He knew he would have to do it soon, before his strength began to ebb and, with it, his resolve. "Maybe early in the morning when I can see better."

Hall was eyeing him in the deepening shadows. "Think you can make it? I'm probably too short and stout to try it," he added.

Jay shrugged. "I don't know what other choice we have. I'll try to get some sleep and then go when it's light enough to see."

"The rocks may be damp and slick early in the morning," Hall said. "And we don't know what time our friends get up," he added, gesturing at the back of the cave.

He had voiced the two fears that Jay had already thought of and tried to put from his mind.

"I wouldn't want to meet them on the trail. But, on the other hand, I don't think that ledge, as far as I could see, is wide enough for a snake to coil for a good strike. Still, I don't want any distractions."

They were silent with their thoughts for a few minutes. Cutter stretched out with his dirty jacket rolled up for a pillow on the hard floor.

"I'd swear those rattlers came down from the ridge above," Jay said, as if to convince himself.

"They were crawling on their bellies," Hall said. "No worry about balancing on two feet."

Jay took a deep breath. "Well, I'm going for it in the morning, regardless. I don't see any other way, except to sit tight, waiting for rescue, and maybe die in here."

That ended the conversation, and they all stretched out at the lower end of the cave to rest.

It was a long, terror-filled night with nightmares of snakes. Jay dreamed he was climbing the outside of the Palace Hotel in San Francisco. Just as he was nearing the top, his hand slipped on a window ledge and he went plunging into space. He could see the carriages and the cobblestone street rushing up at him and he jerked awake in a cold sweat, his own cry of fear ringing in his ears. He didn't know how long he had slept, but he got up, breathing hard, and edged away from the two sleeping forms who stirred uneasily, but did not waken.

He went to the mouth of the cave where he could see millions of stars glittering in the black vault of sky. When he gradually calmed down from the too-realistic dream, he shivered in the chill night breeze that was raking along the face of the cliff. He sat down carefully and let his lower legs hang over the lip of rock. He had heard that all men are born with a fear of heights, but this had never particularly bothered him. Even the balloon flight had been more thrilling than fearful. His own personal fear was one of close, airless places. While in mineshafts, train tunnels, caves, and dense crowds, the demon of claustrophobia had crawled up out of his subconscious to create some unreasoning panic. But if he could get a handhold, he thought he could walk this ledge. If he got to a point where he could go no farther, he could always come back. He just hoped the snakes did not have some sort of underground passage where they were able to slither up to the ridgetop. Well, he would know before long. The moon, if there had been one, had already set, and he thought he could just detect a slight lightening of the night sky. The sun would come up behind the cave so maybe the snakes would not be abroad until the sun was high and the air was warmed. In addition, without the sun directly on the rock wall early in the day to erase the shadows, he could probably pick out the tiny crevices and handholds he would need.

He shivered again as the nightwind penetrated his clothing still damp with sweat.

"Well, wish me luck," Jay said, stripping off his jacket and dropping it on the floor. "If those snakes come out while I'm out there, use my coat to distract them, or knock them over the edge, or whatever you can do," he added, wiping his moist palms on his pants legs. "If I fall, you're on your own. If I make it to the top, I'll get help and be back as soon as I can. I'll holler down from the top if I make it."

"*When* you make it," Hall said, quietly.

It was full daylight, but the sun was still well down behind the ridge, and the forested valley sloping away two hundred feet below the cave was still in deep green shadow.

Jay did not look down as he slipped past the small cedar tree and slid his feet out along the narrow ledge. He worked his fingers carefully into the parallel cracks and seams in the weathered strata at head level as he moved along. Inch by inch and foot by foot he worked his way, glancing alternately at his feet and up at his hands. When he reached the bulge in the wall some thirty feet away from the cave, the foot ledge seemed to disappear, and he paused to survey the situation. The ledge seemed to pass underneath the bulge. If, somehow, he could will his knees to bend backward and keep his toes in the crack, he might be able to make it. Barring that, it looked like a dead end for him.

"What's the matter?" Hall called.

Jay turned his back toward the cave for the first time, scraping his cheek on the bare rock as he did so.

"Can't figure a way around this jutting rock."

He turned his head back to the obstacle. Maybe he could climb over it. He was beginning to breathe a little heavier now as a result of the strain of holding his body flush against the mountain. He tried not to think of what would happen if he slipped. He scrutinized the cracked rock for toeholds.

He looked again to make sure he couldn't somehow squeeze past the hump of rock. Then he took a deep breath and pulled with his fingertips, reaching for a toehold in a small crack. He pushed his body up and felt for another hold for his other foot. His toe scraped naked rock for a second or two and then caught in a tiny irregularity. It wasn't deep enough to hold his weight. The breath was rasping harshly in his throat and sweat trickled down his face, tickling him. He felt desperately for another handhold as fear tightened his stomach. He got the fingers of his left hand into a higher crack and pushed off with his left foot. Then he felt for a spot for his right foot and found one. He clung to the face of the bare rock, gasping, before going on. He was distracted by a shout from the cave, but, in his precarious position, dared not try to look or respond to find out what the yell was about. The hump of rock was almost below him now, and its rounded surface afforded no place to rest.

He moved slowly and carefully, testing each hold. His fingers were aching fearfully from the unaccustomed strain. He shifted his hold twice more and gained another five feet. He was almost over and past the jutting boulder now and he chanced a look down. There was the ledge again, slicing out from under and slanting up toward the unseen ridgetop once more. Sweat was streaming from his face and his heart was pounding, but he felt a moment of elation at seeing it. He began to ease himself back down toward it. He fixed the position of the narrow ledge with his eyes before he began to feel for it with his foot. He let his weight down on his left foot and then, very carefully, his right until he stood on the narrow ledge once more. He wondered briefly what the shout was about, but he was now on the other side of the bulge of rock and out of sight of the cave. And all his attention had to be focused on the task at hand. He stopped for a minute to rest as best he could with his cheek and body pressed against the seamed rock, his feet turned sideways to support his weight. He moved his head slightly so he could glance down to his left at the ledge. He traced it with his eyes as it angled up and away from him. To his relief, it widened out to a foot and then to nearly two feet. If he could just keep a handhold and not look down, his way appeared clear for another ten or twelve yards. And the way the ledge angled upward, he would then be no more than fifteen feet from the top. He was a long way from safety, but his hopes rose slightly. Patience, balance, and concentration would see him to the top of the ridge. A good dose of luck would also help, he thought, taking a deep breath to steady his pounding heart before he proceeded. His hands were beginning to ache from gripping. He removed one hand at a time from the seam of rock just above head level and held his arm down to his side, letting the blood flow back into each hand, flexing his fingers. Only then did he start again. He shifted his weight and slid his left foot carefully.

Just then his fingers touched something alive. He jerked his hand back and nearly threw himself off balance. He teetered on the edge, trying desperately to stay upright. With the fingers of one hand clutching a flat edge, he just did manage to pull his body back against the rock wall, where he stood, his legs quivering, his breath rasping.

Something was up there, just out of sight above head level and he did not dare put his left hand back up. He wanted to remove his right hand from the large crack also, but dared not for fear of falling. He still had to angle his feet to stand on the ledge and he needed at least one handhold to keep him steady. But now he was stuck. In order to move farther, he had to slide his hands along that crack. It was the only way, since the bare rock provided no other seams he could reach that were large enough to get his fingers into. He fought down a cold fear and tried to think. Was there some animal up there? He heard a slight scuffling noise. What had it felt like? He didn't remember feeling fur or feathers. Yet, something had moved and his startled reflex had nearly overbalanced him from his precarious perch. Nothing had flown, and the slight noise told him the thing was still there.

The rock wall had curved outward as he moved along, and he could now feel the early morning sun warming the top of his head. He ran his eyes along the crack and saw that it appeared to pinch downward toward the ledge as it went farther. If he could get past this spot a few feet, he could see where he was putting his hands. Hanging on with his right hand, he moved his left foot as far as he could stretch. Then he let go with his hand and, in one quick motion, grabbed for the seam where it was lower.

As soon as his head came level with the crack, he heard the dreaded buzzing and found himself eye-to-eye with the biggest rattlesnake he had ever seen.

"YYEEEOOOUU!!" Surprise and fear burst from his throat as the snake struck at his face. Jay jerked his head to the left and felt something hit the side of his neck.

Suddenly he was falling, his hands and feet flailing the air, and he knew he was gone.

Then his body slammed to a stop and everything went black.

Chapter Twenty-Three

When Jay heard a faraway voice calling his name, he knew he was in eternity. He was drifting on a dreamy sea, and then could see a far-off light. It was a comforting feeling, and he longed to move toward the warm light above him at the end of the long tunnel, but he could not make himself move. Was this heaven? Was this what it was like to die? It was such a pleasant experience, why would anyone fear it? If he could only reach that soft light!

He heard his name called again, and consciousness began to return. Then the pain in his head and neck told him that he was not dead. He took a shuddering breath and his eyes flickered open and the face of the rock wall swam into view. He struggled to move. He was in the arms of a stunted pine that clung precariously to a seam in the cliff face about twenty feet below the ledge he had fallen from. Once again, a tree had probably saved his life.

Blood was trickling from his mouth where he had bitten his tongue severely and chipped a tooth when his chin had connected with something. He moved slowly and a stabbing pain in his left side made him catch his breath. At least a couple of ribs broken, he guessed. He shakily reached a hand to the side of his neck. There was no blood, no puncture wound;

the skin was smooth and firm. His fingers felt the pulse's steady throbbing. He was bruised and battered, but *alive*.

"Jay McGraw! Can you hear me?" came the voice from above. Someone *was* calling his name! He ripped his shirt loose from a clutching limb. Astride the angled trunk, and holding the prickly needles away from his face, he located the cave above and to his right. Hall and Cutter were peering out of the mouth of the cave, but they were looking up, not down. The pain in his head was severe as he bent his neck back and ran his eyes along the edge of the ridge some fifty feet above him.

"Jay McGraw!" the voice yelled. "Are you hurt?" The voice had a familiar ring to it, but Jay's senses were still somewhat numbed, and the rock wall seemed to be swaying in and out. Then the man moved slightly and Jay spotted the head and shoulders of Vincent Gorraiz.

In spite of his pain and precarious position, relief flooded over Jay, and he breathed a prayer of thanks. He knew Divine Providence had once again spared him for whatever obscure reason.

"I'm all right!" He tried to raise his hand, but the sharp pain in his side stopped the motion halfway.

It took another thirty minutes and much pain to get Jay to the top of the cliff. Gorraiz lowered a rope with a loop in the end of it that Jay slipped one foot into. After numerous stops to rest his ribs, Jay stood weakly at the top, hugging the stocky shepherd with his good right arm.

"God, I'm glad to see you! I won't even ask how you found us until we get Hall and Cutter up here."

By the time the other two men stood with them, and Gorraiz was untying his rope from a nearby tree, the sun was streaming its rays through the foliage of the tall pines on the ridgetop.

"Thought you were a goner," Hall said. "We heard you yell and saw you fall. You hit that little tree so hard it bent like a spring. Lucky it didn't throw you off."

"A dead snag got twisted in my shirt and held me," Jay said.

"You could have been speared like a boiled potato."

Jay nodded. "Instead, it almost caved in my side."

Hall reached over and extracted a thorn from Jay's shirt collar. As he held it up, they both saw it was not a thorn, but a curved, needle-sharp snake fang. Jay felt the blood drain from his face as he stared at it. A half-inch to one side and his carotid artery would have been penetrated. Then, it wouldn't have mattered that the stunted tree had broken his fall.

Hall needed no explanation. "A souvenir," he said, slipping the fang into Jay's shirt pocket. "The rest of him is probably decorating a rock at the foot of that cliff."

"My cousin showed up with a wagonload of supplies just a few hours after you were taken," the bearded shepherd said, coiling the rope. "I told him the story as we unloaded the wagon and put the supplies in the cabin. I also hid your Wells Fargo sacks there in a bag of flour. My cousin is a more peaceable man than I am, and it didn't take long for me to persuade him to look after the flock with the dog while I took his wagon and rifle to come looking for you."

Gorraiz motioned with his head and the four of them started back through the pine grove and down the back side of the ridge toward the road. Jay thought he had never smelled anything as good in all his life as that crisp, pine-scented morning air.

"I knew where Wright's ranch was, but I was fearful of going there in the daylight, so I waited for darkness. I didn't see anyone around, and didn't know what to do next."

"We were locked in the woodshed," Jay interjected.

"I wish I had known that. Anyway, I didn't see any lights, even in the bunkhouse, so I settled down, just out of sight, to wait. I must have fallen asleep, because the next thing I knew, it was morning, and I was just able to slip away without being seen as two men came out of the house. I didn't know what else to do, so I got the wagon where I had hidden it and started toward Rawlings to get help. About fifteen miles away, I ran into a cowboy riding toward Wright's place and was able to capture him with my rifle. I guess I scared him into thinking I was really going to shoot him on the spot, me looking so wild-eyed at him and acting about half-crazy and all." He grinned and winked at them. "But he was riding back from Rawlings and told me everything I wanted to know—that you were captives at Wright's and that the rancher was planning to maroon you in that cave. Well, I had no idea where this cave was, so I just brought him along to show me. We took a roundabout way, and it was away after dark before we got to where the road climbs up this ridge. We stopped there for the night and I tied him up good and tight to the wagon wheel while I slept. Told him I'd cut his throat if he made a sound, although he could have yelled his head off and nobody would have heard him where we were. Anyway, we started up this way at first light and I left him with the wagon and came on up on foot. That's when I saw you fall. It almost made me sick. I thought you were dead at first."

Just then they came down the steep slope into an open meadow and Jay stopped suddenly, staring at the sight of Rafe Coyote-face sitting on the grass, his arms behind him, tied to a wagon wheel. The team of horses was standing patiently in harness, munching on the sparse grass around them. As one moved a step to get a fresh mouthful, the man was saying, "Whoa! Whoa there, boys. Don't move now. That's a good fella. Whoa!"

Gorraiz grinned under his dark beard. "He doesn't know that team's perfectly trained to be ground-reined and won't move more than a couple of feet in any direction. He's afraid if something spooks them, he'll be thumping around on that wheel with a broken neck and legs. It's to his best interest that the team stand still and he remain quiet."

Coyote-face saw them. "Damn you, untie me from this wheel." He was nearly lying on his side as the wheel had turned.

Gorraiz quickly released him, and handed his rifle to Jay to keep the man covered while he retrieved the long lines from under the horses' hooves.

A rifle shot blasted the morning stillness and a slug splintered the corner of the wagon box.

Gorraiz grabbed the heads of the rearing horses.

"Hold it right there!" Jack Bowlegs shouted, stepping out from behind a giant fir tree twenty yards away. They all froze in their tracks. Rafe Coyote-face sprang away from them and snatched his pistol out of Gorraiz's waistband while the shepherd was still clinging to the headstalls of the plunging horses.

"Now then," Bowlegs said as the team was calmed and Gorraiz was able to release them, "we'll take a little walk back up that ridge. It's a damn good thing I came back up here to make sure this morning. That's why I'm the boss's right-hand man. Neither of us likes to leave anything to chance. This time I'll make sure that all of you have a fatal fall from that cliff. And then I'll find a way to get that wagon and team up there and run it off, too, so it'll look like you all went over by accident." He motioned with the rifle. "Get going or I'll shoot you where you stand. Doesn't matter to me. By the time anyone finds your bodies, they'll be picked clean by wolves and buzzards and it'll be hard to tell if a bullet killed you or the fall did."

With a sinking feeling in the pit of his stomach, Jay turned to join the other three as they faced back up the hill.

But he had taken only three or four steps when a shot cracked behind him and he whirled around to see Bowlegs stagger and fall. Coyote-face's pistol spat smoke and flame again and Jack Bowlegs screamed in pain as he grabbed his lower leg. Rafe sprang forward and snatched the wounded man's rifle and threw it into the wagon bed as the horses jumped and plunged away, stepping on their own reins, until they came to a halt a few yards away.

"What are you doing?" Jack screamed.

"That'll hold you until we get far away from here," the shooter replied, calmly, but with his eyes blazing. "I'll not be a party to murder. All I wanted was the money, and you wouldn't even let me take that. Well, damn your hide and Wright's too!"

He turned to the four who were standing, dumbfounded, at this scene. "I'd go with you and tell the sheriff what I know, but I'm in no hurry to see the inside of the Territorial Prison, myself. So I'll just take his horse and ride outa here. I think I hear some greener pastures calling me."

He waved the gun barrel at the man on the ground. "Don't worry about him. He'll live. I was hired because I'm an expert pistol shot. I clipped his collar bone and put a hole in the fleshy part of his calf. He's all yours."

With that he backed away into the shade of the trees on the far side of the mountain meadow, then turned and ran. A few seconds later they heard the thudding of hoofbeats receding.

Jay's head was still reeling from his sudden change of fortune, as Gorraiz led the horses up close and they loaded the bleeding, groaning man into the back of the wagon, after searching him for hidden weapons and confiscating a sheath knife. Then Gorraiz untangled the lines and they climbed aboard. The herder clucked to the team and they rattled down the slope toward the road, leaving dust hanging in the still, morning sunlight.

Chapter Twenty-Four

"I'm still wanted for escaping jail in San Francisco," Marvin Cutter said as the four of them sat in the hotel dining room in Rawlings that afternoon.

"I'll talk to Fred Casey and see if there's any way the judge will give you a lighter sentence," Jay said, trying to chew a piece of antelope steak around a tongue that was still very sore and swollen. After he had said it, he wondered why. Cutter probably did not deserve a lighter sentence. But he dismissed the thought and concentrated on the food—the first he had eaten in two and a half days. In spite of his hunger, he was surprised at how quickly the meat and potatoes were filling him up. Apparently, his stomach had shrunk. "Just don't try to get away from me now," he continued. "I'll have the sheriff here deputize me so I can take you back under arrest."

"You are a lucky man," Gorraiz said, glaring across the table at Cutter. "If my hands had been on your throat two days ago, you would not be sitting here, healthy and eating."

The other three silently turned toward the shepherd whose deep, brown eyes smoldered under the heavy brows.

"But now—huh! I wouldn't dirty my hands on the likes of you," Gorraiz concluded, wiping his mouth and pushing his chair away from the table with an air of finality.

Bowlegs, whose real name turned out to be Jack Larsen, had been turned over to the sheriff who had called for the doctor to treat the man's wounds in his cell. Jay, Fletcher Hall, and Vincent Gorraiz poured out their story to the lawman.

It turned out that the posse that had been sent to look for them and for the train robbers had returned the day before, saddle-sore and empty-handed, having found only the big balloon tangled in the treetops on the mountainside. They had somehow missed Gorraiz's flock, but had been led to the remains of sheep carcasses by the flocks of circling vultures. The sheep had been eaten, scattered, and decomposed so much that the posse only suspected they had been killed by humans.

The posse, composed of about a dozen men—railroaders, merchants and cowmen—and led by only two full-time professional deputies, stopped at Wright's ranchhouse to inquire if the rancher or his men had seen anything. But the rancher had been on his best behavior and professed total ignorance of any strangers in the area or any strange goings-on. He had even invited them in for a drink, but they had politely declined and ridden away, none the wiser.

The main line had been cleared of the disabled locomotive. It had been pulled to Rawlings and now rested in the Union Pacific shop being repaired. A temporary wooden trestle had quickly been constructed by a work crew and the tracks relaid across the wash. Another locomotive had been dispatched to drag the blasted express car out of the way and then had coupled onto the train to haul the delayed and shaken passengers on to Chicago.

As soon as the sheriff heard their story, he sent his two deputies to Wright's ranch to find and arrest the rancher and his men.

The man who had been shot in the raid on the sheep camp lay in a Rawlings hospital, unconscious, with a bullet in his lung. The doctor was giving no assurances of his recovery. The cowboys who had brought him in two days before had told the story that he had shot himself while cleaning his gun.

After leaving the sheriff's office, Jay had gone directly to the Western Union office and sent a telegraph message to Wells Fargo in San Francisco, notifying the home office of his own safety and that of the contents of the express box. Then he had written out a message for the telegrapher to tap over the wire to Fred Casey about the death of Julian Octavian Brown, in case the police did not already know it. He briefly told of the connection between Brown and the stolen gold from the mint.

"If the detectives haven't already made the connection between Brown and that gold, that ought to shake them a little," Jay commented as he paid the telegrapher.

Afterward, the four of them had headed for the hotel dining room and some much-needed food.

When they had finished eating, they all repaired to a local bathhouse where they soaked away the grime and sweat while a Chinese coolie ran their clothes next door to his laundry for a good scrubbing.

Two hours later they emerged, their clothes nearly dry in the windy, dry air, and headed for a tonsorial parlor where all but Gorraiz got shaved. When they came out, smelling of bay rum, Jay felt as if he had rejoined the human race. Even though he was moving very carefully, the pain in his left side had become more severe, so that he could hardly draw a deep breath. It took little persuasion from Hall for Jay to stop by the doctor's white clapboard office. The doctor, James Davis, examined him, feeling gingerly of Jay's side.

"Four broken ribs," was his diagnosis. "Lucky one of them didn't puncture a lung. I want you to take it easy for at least two weeks. You look young and strong. Those ribs should knit fine if you do as I tell you. No unnecessary exertion," he ordered as he finished wrapping clean, white bandages tightly around Jay's rib cage. Jay paid the doctor and left, counting what money he had left from what he had been carrying in his billfold.

"I have enough left for two hotel rooms and about two more meals," he said to Gorraiz as the four of them emerged onto the windswept street once more. "Stop overnight at the hotel with us, and I'll ride back tomorrow to get the two sacks you hid for me."

But the Basque shook his head. "I'm not used to sleeping inside. The wagon will do for me. I would appreciate it if you'd cover the livery stable bill for the team, though."

"Done. And, I don't know about the rest of you, but there's a beer down the street here that has my name on it."

Ten minutes later they sat around a table in a nearly-empty saloon.

"This whole thing is just about cleared up, except for that note nobody can figure out," Jay said, leaning back in his chair.

"I wonder what I can salvage of my balloon," Hall said, almost to himself.

"What were the four words on that note?" Jay continued, ignoring Hall's comment.

"'Palace Windsor Twelve Oaks'," Cutter replied, quoting the cryptic message.

"Any idea what that means?" Jay asked.

They looked blankly at each other.

"Something about the old man's estate, I guess," Cutter said.

"Why do you say that?"

"Brown's estate was known as Twelve Oaks."

Jay sat up in his chair, ignoring the stab of pain in his side. "Why didn't you say so before?"

Cutter shrugged. "Never thought of it until just now. Besides, that's a big estate. I don't know if it means the gold is on the estate."

But Jay was like a hound on the scent now. "Think, man! What could 'Palace Windsor' mean? Did Brown have a private railroad car or something that had that name?"

Cutter shook his head, firmly.

"'Palace Windsor'," Jay repeated. "Sounds like something British."

They sat thinking and sipping at their foamy mugs.

"You worked at the estate for a few months," Jay said to Cutter. "Did you ever see that name on anything?"

Cutter thoughtfully took another gulp and wiped his mouth. "I pretty much had the run of the place, even the main house, but I don't remember that name on anything . . ."

"Did he have a safe in the house that maybe had that brand name?" Hall prompted.

"No."

"I guess they surely would have searched anything as obvious as a safe."

"What about a piece of furniture?"

"Not that I know of."

"Has he got any kin in England?"

Cutter thought a minute. "He never mentioned it. But then, he never said anything to me about his personal life."

"Could it have anything to do with the Palace Hotel in San Francisco? Does he have a suite there called the Windsor?"

No one answered the speculation.

The three of them fell silent once more. Jay was beginning to feel sleepy after his dinner, hot bath, shave, and beer. But he could not let go of this puzzle.

"You know," Cutter finally said after a long silence, "now that I think about it, there was a big, nickel-plated hard coal burning base-burner in his cellar. It was a beautiful thing. Big, fancy. And it had some sort of brand name on it. I remember the letters across the front of it, but I can't remember what they were."

Hall sat up in his chair, suddenly animated. "A base-burner. A base-burner. By God, that's it! I've seen those nickel-plated burners. That's an expensive, fancy model base-burner called Palace Windsor. They're made in a foundry near Buffalo, New York. I remember because there's one of those that heats the depot waiting room at Omaha. I've spent many an hour warming my rear end at it, waiting for trains delayed by blizzards."

"But if that's what the note means, *what* does it mean?"

But Jay McGraw was already out of his chair and halfway to the door. "I'll telegraph San Francisco," he said over his shoulder.

Chapter Twenty-Five

"You still having nightmares about snakes?" Fred Casey asked.

"Only twice since I got back," Jay answered. "I guess it'll pass with time."

It was two weeks later, late on a Sunday morning. Jay and Fred Casey had come directly from church to their favorite restaurant. A chill autumn rain had blown in off the Pacific and was slashing at the windows as they looked out onto the street. Jay's ribs were still wrapped, but he was feeling much better after being given a three-week leave of absence from his job by Wells Fargo.

"That telegram you sent couldn't have come at a better time," Fred said, recounting the details of his amazing discovery. "It almost cost me my job. I rousted the chief out and dragged him back out to that estate, even though his men had been over it with a fine-tooth comb already. We found that base-burner in the cellar all right, and it had the name, 'Palace Windsor' on it, but there was nothing in it or around it. The chief was pretty disgusted and had some harsh words for me. Said I'd play hell making the detective squad if I chased up every blind alley I came to. Then he took off back to town. I was so disgusted, I picked up a chunk of hard coal off the pile and threw it at the stove. I missed, but the coal knocked a chip of paint off the platform the stove was resting on. And, by damn, there was a speck of gold winking at me from under that dull gray paint. I chipped away a little more and I nearly fainted. That old man Brown was as wily as they come. The platform that base-burner was resting on was solid gold! All of it in one big hunk. Brown had used his furnace to somehow melt that million and a half in double eagles and poured the liquid gold into a wooden mold, let it cool, and painted it gray and set the base-burner on top of it. Probably had the help of the old Chinese houseman who was killed later by the tong. Well, as you know, that not only put me back in good graces with the chief, but I'm now a member of the detective squad. No more walking a night beat in Chinatown for me. And the pay is better, too."

"Not to mention the headlines you've gotten," Jay added with a grin.

"You know, between the two of us, we've helped account for the recovery of the whole three million that was stolen from the mint about eighteen months ago," Fred said. He spread some grape jam on a piece of bread, popped it into his mouth, and leaned back in his chair.

"What happened to the gardener who brought the message to the Wells Fargo office?" Jay inquired after a few moments.

"He never turned up. Just vanished. Brown's cook told us he was a young fellow named Otto Anderson who was from Missouri. No family here that anybody knows of."

"Could be he's hiding out if he's afraid. Or maybe he left town."

"More likely at the bottom of the bay if the tong got hold of him. And they must have caught up with him because they found out what he did with the message."

"It's strange how things turn out. He's probably the real hero in all this, but we may never know anything more about him than his name."

"Never found Julian Octavian Brown, either," Casey said. "Can't start a murder investigation until we know for a fact somebody's been killed. No bodies; no witnesses. You can bet if the tong's responsible, their bodies will never be found.

"The Chicago police did locate Simpson, the man Brown's note was addressed to. Fortunately, they got to him at his office just in time. Some Orientals had been asking for him at the Excelsior Hotel and were lounging around in the hallways near his suite that day. Simpson is president of the Mercantile Bank. He's denied knowing anything about stolen gold. He admits knowing Brown and making two joint investments with him, but that's all. The police will press the investigation, but my guess is they'll never be able to prove any link or complicity, if there is any, unless they can come up with some letters, telegrams or written records."

"I just thought of something else," Jay said. "How can the government legally confiscate that gold if it can't be identified as coming from the mint?"

Casey smiled. "They can't, but they did. Technically, they are only holding it at the mint temporarily while the investigation is continuing."

"What investigation?"

"They are attempting to find witnesses who may have seen the tong men at the estate, trying to find Otto Anderson, going over the records at Brown's bank and home, looking for Brown's body and trying to pick up the trail of Jacob Wright. The only information we have that Brown is dead is what you told us Jacob Wright said, and Wright eluded the posse. Several of his men were picked up, but they were apparently only hired hands and weren't privy to all the inside information about the tong's activities. Marvin Cutter gave a rather vague description of the Orientals he saw at Brown's estate. He was too scared at the time to take a really good look.

"We've already had two men, who claim to be relatives of Brown's from Chicago, putting in their bid for the gold and Brown's estate. There was no will that can be found. This thing could be tied up in court for years, especially if Brown's body isn't found so he can be declared dead right away. It's going to be a real mess, I'm afraid." He paused to refill his coffee cup.

"You mentioned Marvin Cutter. Have you seen him lately?"

"As a matter of fact, I have. Would you believe he's actually trying to go straight? Since the judge gave him a suspended sentence and probation, he's been working hard."

"Maybe he was inspired by Fletcher Hall," Jay mused. "You know how slick a pickpocket he is. He's one of the best I've ever seen. His hands have the talent to be a very good magician."

"Wonders never cease," Jay said, shaking his head. "I'm glad for him. He wasn't really a bad man."

"Too bad that Jacob Wright got away," Fred said.

"Yeah, but he's on the run and won't cause any more trouble for a while. And Gorraiz can rest easier, too, since Wright was the one spearheading the drive, through the Cattlemen's Association, to force the sheepmen out by violence."

"Fletcher Hall's probably making hay from all this," Jay remarked.

"You're right. I saw a piece in the newspaper yesterday where he was lecturing in St. Louis to raise money for construction of another balloon. According to the reporter, Hall was not only thrilling the audiences with all the details of his wild adventure, but was also billing himself as the main character in the drama."

"Of course. What else could you expect from him?"

"Let me take another look at that watch you got," Casey said. "Someday you can show it to your grandchildren to prove that you were a hero at least once."

Jay pulled the gold-plated watch from his vest pocket, unhooked the chain and handed it across the table.

Casey popped open the back of the case and held it to the light. The ornate inscription read:

"From Wells Fargo & Company to Messenger Jay McGraw. In token of his courageous and successful defence of the Express Car against Highway Robbers near Burning Rock Cut, Wyoming Territory, October 3, 1883."

SWIFT THUNDER

Tim Champlin

Lance Barlow is only nineteen when he starts riding with a Missouri militia group known as the Border Ruffians. He joins them seeking adventure, but their wanton destruction and murder of the Free-Staters is too much for him. Finally, after a brutal attack on a farm family, Lance can't take any more. He rebels and switches sides. He reunites with his best friend, a freed slave named Shadrack, and together the pair set off to ride with the newly organized Pony Express. But Lance gets more adventure than he bargained for when he is forced to rescue Shadrack from slavers. Still working for the Pony Express, the friends escape west to Utah, with the Missouri militia and a Marysville slaver on their trail. They have no idea that the real danger lies in front of them, waiting in the midst of Paiute country.

___4758-6 $4.50 US/$5.50 CAN

Dorchester Publishing Co., Inc.
P.O. Box 6640
Wayne, PA 19087-8640

Please add $1.75 for shipping and handling for the first book and $.50 for each book thereafter. NY, NYC, and PA residents, please add appropriate sales tax. No cash, stamps, or C.O.D.s. All orders shipped within 6 weeks via postal service book rate. Canadian orders require $2.00 extra postage and must be paid in U.S. dollars through a U.S. banking facility.

Name_____
Address_____
City_____ State_____ Zip_____
I have enclosed $_____ in payment for the checked book(s).
Payment <u>must</u> accompany all orders. ❏ Please send a free catalog.
    CHECK OUT OUR WEBSITE! www.dorchesterpub.com

MAN ON A RED HORSE

FRED GROVE

Jesse Wilder is a man who has seen more than his share of violence. A former captain in the Army of Tennessee, he is inducted into the Union army as a "galvanized Yankee" after the Battle of Shiloh. After the war he heads to Mexico to fight with the Juaristas against Emperor Maximilian. That costs him the life of his wife and his unborn child. All he wants then is peace. But instead he is offered a position as a scout on a highly secret mission into Mexico, where bandits are holding the Sonora governor's daughter for ransom. The rescue attempt is virtually a suicide mission; the small group is vastly outnumbered and is made up of men serving time in the garrison jail. Jesse has every reason to walk away from the offer—but he can't. Not when one of his wife's murderers is second in command to the Sonoran bandit chief.

_4771-3 $4.50 US/$5.50 CAN

Graciela of the Border

John Duncklee

Jeff Collins knows horses. He works as a horse trainer on the Sierra Diablo ranch in Arizona, and he is mighty good at it. But he wants more. He's dreamed for years of having his own ranch. He sees his chance when he wins a blue roan in a high-stakes poker game. This isn't just any roan; it is carrying the foal of a great racehorse, and that foal is Jeff's ticket to his dreams. When that roan is stolen and herded along with other horses toward the Mexican border, Jeff knows where he has to go. But he doesn't know what will be waiting for him when he gets there. The border is a dangerous place, a harsh land filled with bandits and outlaws—and the woman who will change his life . . . Graciela of the border.

___4809-4 $4.99 US/$5.99 CAN

River Walk

Rita Cleary

Many accounts have been written of the historic expedition led by Meriwether Lewis and William Clark across North America, but author Rita Cleary offers the story from a very different point of view—through the eyes of John Collins, who is persuaded to join the expedition by his friend, a hunter who will supply meat for the voyagers. Of all the risks of the journey, both natural and man-made, perhaps none will prove as dangerous for Collins as his love for Laughing Water, a young Mandan widow with a child. Lewis and Clark's pact with the members of the expedition strictly forbids desertion for any reason. For Collins, his sworn oath becomes not only a question of honor, but a matter of life and death.

___4922-8 $4.50 US/$5.50 CAN

TREASURES OF THE SUN
T. V. OLSEN

The lost city of Huacha has been a legend for centuries. It is believed that the Incas concealed a fantastic treasure there before their empire fell to Francisco Pizarro's conquistadores in the 16th century. So when Wilbur Tennington comes upon a memoir written by one of Pizarro's men, revealing the exact location of Huacha, visions of gold fill his eyes. He wastes no time getting an expedition together, then sets out on his quest. He should have known, though, that nothing so valuable ever comes easily. He will have to survive freezing mountain elevations, volcanic deserts, tribes of headhunters, and murderous bandits if he hopes to ever find the...treasures of the sun.

___4904-X $4.50 US/$5.50 CAN

Behold a
Red Horse
Cotton Smith

After the Civil War, Ethan Kerry carved out the Bar K cattle spread with little more than hard work and fierce courage—and the help of his younger, slow-witted brother, Luther. But now the Bar K is in serious trouble. Ethan's loan was called in and the only way he can save the spread is if he can drive a herd from central Texas to Kansas. Ethan will need more than Luther's help this time—because Ethan has been struck blind by a kick from an untamed horse. His one slim hope has come from a most unlikely source—another brother, long thought dead, who follows the outlaw trail. Only if all three brothers band together can they save the Bar K . . . if they don't kill each other first.

___4894-9 $4.99 US/$5.99 CAN

Dorchester Publishing Co., Inc.
P.O. Box 6640
Wayne, PA 19087-8640

Please add $2.50 for shipping and handling for the first book and $.75 for each book thereafter. NY and PA residents, please add appropriate sales tax. No cash, stamps, or C.O.D.s. All orders shipped within 6 weeks via postal service book rate. Canadian orders require $2.50 extra postage and must be paid in U.S. dollars through a U.S. banking facility.

Name_____
Address_____
City_____ State_____ Zip_____
I have enclosed $_____ in payment for the checked book(s).
Payment <u>must</u> accompany all orders. ❑ Please send a free catalog.
    CHECK OUT OUR WEBSITE! www.dorchesterpub.com

THE
OUTLAWS
WAYNE D.
OVERHOLSER

Del Delaney has been riding for the same outfit for ten years. Everything seems fine...until the day he is inexplicably charged with rape by the deputy sheriff. Del knows he is innocent, but the deputy's father is the local judge, so he does a desperate thing—he escapes and leaves the state. He drifts until he runs out of money and meets up with two other wanted men in Colorado. Since he is wanted himself, he figures he can do worse than throw in with them. But these men are wanted for a reason and before he knows it, Del is getting in over his head—and helping to organize a bank robbery.

___4897-3 $3.99 US/$4.99 CAN